Aquarius

Emily Martha Sorensen

Also by Emily Martha Sorensen

Wicked Witches of Restva:
Black Magic Academy
White Magic Academy

The End in the Beginning:
The Keeper and the Rulership
The Fires of the Rulership
The Magic or the Rulership (prologue)

Comics:
A Magical Roommate
To Prevent World Peace

Picture Books:
Tabby, Tabby, Burning Bright

Short Story Collections:
Worlds of Wonder
Magic and Mischief
Tales of Tie-Ins

Fairy Senses:
Fairy Eyeglasses
Fairy Compass
Fairy Earmuffs
Fairy Barometer
Fairy Pox
Fairy Slippers
Fairy Lunchbox
Fairy Icepack
Fairy Stopwatch
Fairy Toothbrush
Fairy Perfume
Fairy Crown

Dragon Eggs:
Dragon's Egg
Dragon's Hope
Dragon's First Christmas
Dragon's Fire
Dragon's Song
Dragon's First Valentine

Trilogy of a Teenage Werevulture:
Trials of a Teenage Werevulture
Trifles of a Teenage Werevulture

Weredodo Cozy Mysteries:
Weredodo Sleuth

The Numbers Just Keep Getting Bigger:
Twenty-Four Potential Children of Prophecy

Magical Mayhem:
To Prevent World Peace
To Prevent Chic Costumes
To Prevent Clear Paths
To Prevent Smart Choices
To Prevent Warm Welcomes
To Prevent Cute Mascots
To Prevent First Place (prologue)
To Prevent Fresh Starts
To Prevent New Allies
To Prevent Best Friends
To Prevent Good Luck

The Virgo Curse:
Not Quite a Curse
Not Quite a Blessing
Not Quite Changed

http://www.emilymarthasorensen.com

To Ben,
my husband,
who taught me what love is.

Chapter 1

To See a Soul

Amanda's open pencil case fell off her desk and spilled all over the floor, so she got down on her hands and knees to clean it up. Trying to stand, she whammed her head against the bottom of her desk.

Owwww! Amanda gripped the top of her head with tears in her eyes.

"Are you okay?" the guy with the desk next to her asked, leaning over and offering his hand to help her up.

Amanda looked up, and she saw his eyes. They were filled with genuine concern and kindness. She reached out and took his hand, and he helped her up.

Her throbbing head forgotten, she thought, *Wow, I wish I knew him better,* and then something else exploded across her sight.

She saw a cluster of tall buildings, each a marvel of architectural construction. They shone in the dim light of a setting sun, each one different and each beautiful, the view marred only by an invasion of black clouds encroaching from the distance.

What? Amanda's breath caught in her throat.

She realized she was still holding the guy's hand. She rapidly let go and sat down at her desk, heart pounding.

What had that been? Her imagination? But the sight was still so vivid in her memory. She knew without being told that the cityscape had been symbolic. But of what?

And could she do it again?

Amanda closed her eyes and thought, *I want to see that again.* Then she opened her eyes.

In front of her was a stream that crashed down into a waterfall. Off to the right was a field of flowers with baby animals scampering around. Behind her was a confused jumble that reminded her of Cubism. And off to the left . . .

There it was. There was the cityscape again.

What's it symbolic of? she wondered.

The answers came as soon as she asked.

Each of the buildings represented something different, something precious that had been built with great care. A pale cream one with lattices and decks on every floor was kindness. A deep forest green one with rows of columns was patience. A gleaming silver one with long, striped windows was knowledge. A luminous blue one that was lit up by a thousand yellow lanterns was gentleness.

It's a person, Amanda realized. Her heart was in her throat. *I'm seeing a person.*

The vision winked out as soon as she stopped paying attention to it, and she realized she'd been staring at the boy beside her for a long time. He was glancing over at her with a questioning look on his face.

Amanda's face heated up, and she looked to the front of the classroom, chewing on her lower lip nervously. She'd just been staring at a *person* like that? And she was sure what she had just seen was accurate, too. Talk about an invasion of privacy!

Oh, but . . . she wanted to look at that cityscape again. It was so beautiful. She wished she had a canvas right now to capture it.

Who was he, anyway? The guy beside her? It was the first day of the second semester of her senior year, her first day at a new school, and she didn't know anyone. Her friends were all far away.

To See a Soul

It was a terrible time to have moved, but her dad had been offered a new job in a new town at triple his previous salary, only under the condition that he start right away. After talking it over with Amanda and her mother, they'd determined that it was too good of an opportunity to miss, so they'd packed up their house over Christmas vacation and gotten here just in time for Amanda to start the second semester at her new school.

Logically, of course, it had been the right thing to do. Amanda would be going off to college in less than a year, so it wasn't like she would have seen her friends for much longer anyway, and her father had promised to use his increased salary to pay for her tuition, as well as to pay off her older brothers' student loans, so that the three of them wouldn't have to start out their adult lives in crushing debt.

By any measure, it would have been stupid to tell her dad not to take the job, even though her parents had given the final choice to her. It would have also been selfish, since her brothers would be benefiting as much as her. So she'd agreed, and hadn't complained, and now she was in a new school where she knew nobody at all.

A new school, in a new class, sitting next to a boy who had a beautiful soul.

Amanda's face heated up again, and she clenched her fists on her lap as the bell rang and the teacher got up from his desk and started lecturing about the Roman Empire.

What was his name, anyway? The guy sitting next to her? Should she ask? Did she dare? He was probably popular, since he was physically attractive and so nice that it made her heart melt. Did he have a girlfriend? Did she dare ask *that?*

She didn't manage to take a single note, or even hear much the teacher said. Her mind was too busy churning.

At last, the bell rang.

Amanda scrambled to gather up her textbook, notebook, and pencil case full of pens that she hadn't so much as uncapped, even to doodle. She glanced over at the boy sitting off to her left, hopefully casually. "Hi. I'm Amanda. What's your name?"

"Alex." His voice was quiet.

"Nice to meet you, Alex."

"You, too." He smiled and nodded, then gathered up his things and left the classroom.

Argh! Amanda buried her heated face in her hands. *I have to find out if he has a girlfriend! But I don't want to ask! Aaaarrghhh!*

The answer to that question would make all the difference as to whether she was glad she'd just moved into this school or not.

〰〰

Amanda held her tray and looked around the cafeteria at the many tables filled with students, most of them in groups that were chatting and laughing.

She'd been one of those people just a few weeks ago. She'd had friends from church and early morning seminary. Now, she was isolated.

She could, perhaps, have tried to join one of those groups. But when she didn't know anybody? That seemed presumptuous at best, and pesky at worse.

She chose a table off in a corner that no one was sitting at, and started to eat her lunch alone.

It was sad and depressing. Perhaps she should have brought one of her textbooks and studied during lunch. If she started doing that every day, it would brand her as a nerd and ensure no one talked to her, but maybe social isolation for her last few months of high school would be a good thing. She had SATs coming up, after all.

A tray plonked down across from her. Amanda looked up.

A Hispanic girl with long black hair and a prominent nose waved at her and sat down.

Amanda breathed a sigh of relief. "Hi. I'm Amanda. Who are you?"

The girl held up a finger, opened a large purse slung over her shoulder, and pulled out a notebook. She flipped to the first page and held it out.

In large block letters, it said: *My name is Valerie.*

Amanda blinked. "You can't talk?"

The girl rolled her eyes and nodded.

"Are you deaf?"

The girl shook her head. Then she flipped to the second page, which said: *I can't explain it. It's weird.*

Amanda was taken aback. Apparently Valerie had been asked this before.

"Well, it's nice to meet you," Amanda tried.

The girl beamed and flipped through a few pages. She turned the notebook around. *It's nice to meet you, too.*

This was a little eerie.

"Can you . . . see the future or something?" Amanda asked cautiously.

Valerie looked very amused. She shook her head. Thankfully, she didn't seem to have a prepared notebook answer.

"I'm new," Amanda said. "You probably noticed."

Valerie smiled and shrugged.

"I just moved in," Amanda said. "My dad got a new job here."

Valerie held up a finger and flipped through her notebook to nearly a back page. She held it out. *Do you know what we have in common?*

Amanda was baffled. "Uh . . . nothing?"

Valerie hung in her head in obvious frustration.

"We're both students here?" Amanda tried.

Valerie waved her hand in the *go on* sign.

"You're a new student, too?"

Valerie shrugged and waved her hand again.

"I don't know, Valerie. I'm sorry. Can you write it down?"

Valerie flipped to a page near the front of her notebook. *I can't write anything new.*

"What?!" Amanda was completely mystified now. "Why not?"

Valerie flipped back to nearly the beginning. *I can't explain it. It's weird.*

"Can you get somebody else to write it down for you?"

Valerie shook her head. Then she flipped to another page that said: *I don't know.*

"Well, which is it?"

Valerie's shoulders slumped. She rolled her eyes up at the ceiling and then shook her head.

"So . . . you *can't* get somebody else to write it down for you?"

Valerie nodded and held up a finger. She flipped through her notebook, holding her previous place, returned to: *Do you know what we have in common?* and then flipped immediately back to *I don't know.*

"Ohhh!" Amanda cried in realization. "You don't know what it is, either!"

Valerie nodded, looking pleased.

"But . . . then what makes you think we *have* something in common?"

Valerie flipped back to nearly the start again. *I can't explain it. It's weird.*

Amanda had the creeping suspicion that this was some kind of prank.

"Well, I have no idea what you're talking about," she said cautiously, trying to be polite in case this wasn't a practical joke. "Why don't you come back when you know what it is?"

Valerie thumped her head on the table over and over again.

"I really can't," Amanda said in a softer tone. "I have no clue what you're talking about."

Valerie breathed in deeply, breathed out again, and shrugged. She got up, tossed the notebook in her enormous purse, waved, and got up and walked off, leaving her tray of uneaten food behind.

Well, that was probably the most confusing conversation I've ever had, Amanda thought, unsettled. *What is up with that girl?*

A thought rose up in her head.

I could find out.

Before she could talk herself out of it, Amanda closed her eyes and thought, *I want to know what's up with that girl,* and then opened them. In the direction she had seen the silent girl retreating, she now saw a dozen different visions from a dozen students. She had no clue which one was Valerie.

Off in the corner of her eye, she saw the cityscape.

Amanda spun around in that direction, the visions extinguished, and she saw Alex sitting on his own at a different table.

On his own. Not with a whole group.

Amanda's heart pounded. She stood up, picked up her tray, and walked over to his nearly empty table.

"Can I sit here?" she asked in a shaking voice.

Alex looked up and smiled at her. "Sure."

Amanda sat down across from him, biting her lip with fear and excitement, and picked up her spoon to forge into the mashed potatoes that were cold by now on her tray.

He probably didn't have a girlfriend if he was sitting alone at lunchtime. Right?

Chapter 2

The Smell of Connections

Valerie hadn't talked for over three months. She was sick and tired of it.

It wasn't that she was shy. She *loved* to talk, she *loved* to meet people, and she *loved* to have her nose in everyone else's business all the time.

Literally.

So not talking for months was an absolute torture. But she could only smell connections when she wasn't talking, and the longer she took without talking, the further her range stretched. It usually stretched at a rate of about six-tenths of a mile per day.

So right now, her range stretched out to at least sixty miles. And once she broke her silence, she would have to start all over again with a range of only a few inches.

But I may have found what I was looking for, at last!

Valerie skipped on the way to her van, which was a beat-up old clunker parked well past Greenfell High School because its parking lot was full. If she had found the thing she wanted, maybe she would finally be able to start talking again.

The Smell of Connections

Boy, did she miss it!

She wasn't a student here. She wasn't a student anywhere. She'd graduated from high school awhile ago. She was nineteen, and she'd spent the last year and a half on the road. She loved being a nomad, but she missed having connections.

It didn't necessarily matter what kind. A close friend she could call up from a distance would be great. A boyfriend would be even better. Maybe even blood relatives.

Not that genes necessarily meant anything. If they did, she wouldn't have left in the first place.

What she wanted was a bunch of strong connections that wouldn't disappear within a week of not seeing her. Connections that mattered. Connections that most people took for granted. It would probably be easier to forge some if she stayed in one place, but she didn't want to stay in one place. She wanted people who would miss her.

And she may have found that here.

Maybe.

If nothing else, she'd definitely found something . . . weird.

Valerie unlocked her van, hopped into the driver's side, and slammed the door.

The front of her van wasn't too bad, only littered with a dozen notebooks and a hundred or so fast food wrappers, but the back of the van was a disaster area. There were no seats back there, just a big empty space filled with a sea of dirty laundry, loose pens, dozens of notebooks, her sleeping bag and pillow, and about a thousand fast food wrappers piled up in strata that went back months.

I should probably clean it up sometime, Valerie thought vaguely. During the times when she was talking, she usually cleaned her van about once a week, but whenever she wasn't, she tended to think it wasn't worth the bother.

She *did* put forth the effort to look presentable at all times, though. Cute clothes, makeup, and she had a YMCA membership so she could shower at a nearby one regularly. You never knew when you might meet whoever-you-were-looking-for, after all.

Valerie's stomach growled, reminding her that she'd ditched her lunch at the school cafeteria.

"That was stupid," she muttered to herself. "Wasting perfectly good food just because you were mad."

She talked to herself sometimes. It kept her sane during the times she couldn't talk to other people. For whatever reason, talking to herself didn't break her range. She could also sing along with her music as long as there was nobody else in the van. Good thing, or she really *would* go insane.

She turned her key in the ignition, put on her seat belt, and drove around, keeping her eyes peeled for fast food restaurants. She found a plethora of them near another high school on the other side of town, so she went into a Wendy's, ordered a few burgers by pointing at the menu, and parked near the sidewalk to munch while she wrote.

She couldn't write new words to communicate during the times she wasn't talking. That would also break her range. But she could write new words for herself, so she did.

Valerie rummaged through a box of notebooks on the floor between the seats until she found the one she was looking for. Then she put her feet up on the passenger's side seat, dug a pen out of the glove compartment, unwrapped a cheeseburger, and munched it while she started taking notes in tiny handwriting that was illegible to anyone except her.

Found the source of the unnamed smell, she scribbled down. *Still don't know how to define it. Reminds me of the shared-suffering connection, but it's not quite the same.*

She couldn't describe connections in terms of normal odors. They weren't floral or sweet or sour or anything else that normal people could smell. She usually resorted to describing new ones in terms of other connection smells that were similar.

For her own reference, anyway. Bizarrely, she could never talk about what she smelled to anyone else, even during the times she was talking and didn't have range to preserve.

There were even certain words that seemed to be forbidden under any circumstances.

The Smell of Connections

Words like "smell." Or "scent." Or "connections."

She couldn't say any of those when she was trying to talk to another person. She couldn't even write them. But when talking to herself or writing for herself, she could use any words she wanted. She wished she knew why. It was so weird.

Valerie glanced up through the windshield as she took another bite of her cheeseburger, and she caught sight of a hot African-American guy walking down the sidewalk toward her. She grinned, enjoying the view for a second, and then went back to her notebook.

I was right when I counted them yesterday. There are a total of twenty-eight connections within my range with the exact same smell and strength, Valerie wrote. *Seven of them are connected with me. This implies that there are eight people within my range, including me, who all have the same connection with each other. The question is, what is it?*

She took a bite of her cheeseburger and watched the hot guy stop to chat with a pretty girl who was carrying a backpack. There was a mutual-attraction connection between those two, no surprise there.

Greenfell High School had three of those connections within the building, and three that stretched out of it to connect with me, which implies there are three people there. I found two of them today. There was a boy student who was polite but wouldn't answer questions, and then a girl student called Amanda who

She stopped abruptly, her pen hovering over the notebook. There was a brand new mutual-attraction connection nearby that was connected with . . . her.

She glanced up and saw the hot guy looking her way. He waved and then sauntered off.

It's him!!

She shoved the pen into the notebook, tossed her notebook into the box, and flung the car door open.

He walked with a swagger, which was a trait that every guy she'd ever crushed on had in common. He also had the dark skin that she liked better than light skin.

Valerie jumped out the car, slammed the door, and sniffed as fast as possible for other information.

He had no mutual-romantic-love or mutual-crush connections, which was important, because there was no point in chasing after a guy who had a girlfriend.

He had over a hundred current mutual-attraction connections, which was annoying, but no surprise; first of all, he was gorgeous, and second, if he'd formed one with Valerie just by glancing at her, he'd probably done the same with a whole lot of other girls.

He had three blood-relative and family-love connections within her range, which was a good sign that he had a happy home life. That was important because she wasn't looking for a repeat of the situation she'd left.

There were no enemy connections, aside from a few dozen mutual-rivalry ones, which was pretty common for guys and not a source of concern.

Most importantly of all, he didn't have any had-sex-with-this-person-before connections, which was aggravatingly *uncommon* among the guys she found attractive. She always liked the ones with way more self-confidence than sense.

So in other words, he was exactly what she was looking for. And this was a place she might be staying for awhile. And he was rapidly walking away.

She quickly weighed the risks and rewards of talking to him.

She didn't know if she was missing any important information. Her nose wasn't infallible, since she couldn't smell any connections with people outside her range. Sixty miles was pretty far in all directions; that covered about a sixth of the entire state. Still, there was always the possibility that he had a long-distance girlfriend or something, which would be a major bummer. She would hate to give up her range for no reason.

Maybe she could hold on to her silence longer and stalk him in order to gather more intel before talking? But her range was so wide right now that stalking him probably wouldn't tell her anything new, and it would definitely creep him out if he noticed, which he probably would.

The Smell of Connections

She could try to hit on him without talking, but trying to flirt through pre-written notebooks was almost certain to break the mutual attraction and make him think she was weird.

Meanwhile, mutual-attraction connections faded rapidly when they weren't strengthened by repeated contact; the smell from this one was already dwindling. If she waited much longer, he'd forget her entirely, and she might not be able to find him again.

So, was it worth losing her range to talk to him right now?

Well . . .

I've found two of the three at Greenfell already, Valerie rapidly evaluated. *I'll have eight hours of silence built up when I wake up tomorrow, which is several buildings' worth of range, so I should be able to find the third without a problem, no matter what.*

That leaves the four other people spread all over my range. A few days of silence and some driving around would be enough to smell every single connection in the whole town. Even if the rest are scattered across other nearby towns, assuming that the unnamed connection doesn't fade over time, I can find them all within a few weeks, guaranteed.

That meant her silence was disposable at this point.

Valerie took a deep breath, thought mournfully, *Three months of range!* and then ran after the guy, who was waiting for the crosswalk light to turn at the end of the street.

She caught up with him just as the light changed, walked across the street after him, and then said casually as they reached the other side, "Hi, I'm Valerie. Who're you?"

The odors vanished from around her. The air was eerily empty, devoid of all the constant information and distractions she'd been building up for months now.

The African-American guy turned around. He was tall, had short hair, wore a denim jacket, and had a cocky smile that she loooooooooved.

"Caleb," he said, looking her up and down. "Are you new at school?"

Argh, he's still in high school? That means he's at least a year younger than me!

That wasn't a dealbreaker for Valerie, but it might be for him. Better get it out of the way and find out if she'd given up her range for nothing.

"No, I'm nineteen," she said casually. "I graduated the year before last. I'm not a student anywhere now. I'm a nomad."

"Really?" His eyes lit up. "That sounds so cool! Are you, like, permanently traveling?"

His excitement was infectious. "Yeah!" Valerie said. "I go to every museum and state park I can find. Or I just get out and walk down hiking trails sometimes. I love amusement parks too, but they're really expensive, so I only go when I'm enough under the budget to justify it. I have a zillion photos on my phone now."

And she had no one to share them with, but there was no point in saying that.

"That's sooooooo coooooooool," Caleb moaned. "I've never even been on a family vacation."

"Wow, really? Why not?"

"My dad," Caleb griped.

"Is he sick?"

"Yeah, in a manner of speaking. Travel makes it worse, so he's against it. He even made me quit sports because he didn't like how excited I got about going to away games."

"Ugh." Valerie grimaced. Maybe his family was dysfunctional. That wouldn't be good. "Sounds unfair."

"Well, he's just trying to watch out for me," Caleb said quickly. "He's not *wrong*. It's just — I hate that he's right."

"Hmm." Valerie looked at him speculatively. Well, why not? She liked him so far. "Are you allowed to go hiking?"

"I dunno," he said, a grin growing on his face. "Why?"

"'Cause I found a pretty cool hiking trail about half an hour's drive that way." She pointed off to the east. "I could take you. If you want."

"That would be cool!" Caleb said. "Can we do it on Saturday? I won't tell my dad where we're going. I'll just say it's a date."

"Does that mean it *is* a date?" she asked shrewdly.

"Yeah!" He paused. "Unless you don't want it to be."

"'Course I want it to be," she declared. "You ever look in a mirror? You're hot."

He burst out laughing. "You think so?"

"Duh!" she said, twirling a finger through a curl of her hair. "And I'm sure you know. Nobody looks that good by accident."

"Well, maybe I put in some effort," he said with a grin.

She didn't bother to ask if he thought she was hot, too. She already knew that he did. She pulled out her phone and opened her calendar. "Okay, where are we meeting, and what time?"

"Here at nine am okay?"

"Sure." Valerie typed it in with her thumbs. "Got a time when you need to be back home?"

"My curfew's ten. You think we'll be out that long?"

"If you don't get tired. I usually spend all day when I go out hiking. I need the exercise so I don't turn into a blob. That's the downside of sitting in a car all day."

"Sounds a lot better than sitting in school all day." Caleb made a face. "I've got senioritis so bad, I could just scream."

"You planning to go to college?" Valerie asked him.

"I dunno. You?"

"Not really. Too expensive."

"And you've already got a reason to leave your hometown," Caleb said enviously.

Wasn't a home, Valerie thought. "And I should get your number in case anything comes up."

"Oh, yeah." Caleb pulled out his phone. "I'll get yours, too."

Valerie made a show of typing his number in for longer than she needed to, so that she had an excuse to keep her mouth shut for over a minute. That gave her two and a half feet of extra range, so she could smell what was between them right now.

Physical attraction, emotional attraction, friendship . . . cool! They're all weak right now, but that's a good start.

She was excited for Saturday.

Chapter 3

The Words Not Spoken

For the next few days, Amanda sat across from Alex at his lunch table without asking. He didn't object, just smiled at her whenever she sat down. They caught each other's eyes and smiled at each other in the hallways, too.

She really, *really* hoped he didn't have a girlfriend. Maybe one of these days, she'd get up the nerve to ask.

Since she didn't have friends to hang out with, she had a lot of time to paint at home, too. She hung the four canvases she was currently working on across her bedroom wall, so they were easy to pull down and put on her easel whenever she felt like it.

The one that was closest to finished was the painting of her parents to give them on their anniversary, so she mostly focused on that one. She only let herself work on four projects at once, since she would never finish anything if she let herself start a new painting whenever she felt like it.

She knew exactly what she wanted to work on next, and she tingled with anticipation whenever she thought about it. It was going to be the cityscape she saw when she looked at Alex.

The Words Not Spoken

She wasn't sure why she kept getting those visions, but they were fascinating, so she didn't mind them. She'd figured out how to turn them on and off whenever she wanted now, so she often peeked at Alex while he wasn't looking to decide what colors she would mix to paint each building.

Once she was done with the painting of her parents, then she would start sketching the buildings, and figure out what angle she wanted to paint them from. She couldn't wait to begin.

On late Friday afternoon, while she was deeply absorbed in filling in the tiny squares of navy blue on her mom's gingham dress in the painting, her father walked into the room and said, "Are you ready to go?"

"Huh?" Amanda looked up.

"Remember? One of my coworkers invited us over for dinner? We said we'd come on Friday?"

"Oh." Amanda vaguely recalled that. She looked down at her paint-smeared fingers. "Maybe I should get changed."

"Maybe you should," her father chuckled. "Don't take too long. It would be better not to be late."

Amanda nodded and got up, not complaining even though she felt a pang of regret. She wasn't done yet! She'd expected to have hours more to work on this!

She carefully put her paints away, then went to the bathroom to wash her hands. When she returned, she hung the painting back on the wall, where it would be ready for the next time she wanted to add to it, removed the smock, and exchanged her ratty T-shirt and oldest jeans for a pretty floral print dress.

She touched up her make-up in the mirror quickly, which didn't take long, since she only wore a little bit anyway. She also gave her lips a good dosage of lip gloss, because they were dry and cracked again. She really had to learn to stop chewing on them.

When she got to the living room, her mom was straightening her dad's tie and teasing him. "Remember, if you get food on it, I'll have to give you a replacement one for Christmas!"

"Please spare me," Amanda's dad moaned. "I think I have a hundred and fifty ties from the kids."

"Ready to go?" Amanda's mom asked, looking at her.

She nodded.

"It's a shame they can't meet Joseph and Wallace," Amanda's dad said. "From what Steven's told me about his son, the three of them would probably get along."

"Teenager?"

"Just turned eighteen."

"A few months older than Amanda, huh?" Her mom flicked a teasing glance over at her. "Maybe *they'll* get along."

Amanda's face felt hot. *I already have a boy I like, thank you!*

Not that she'd told her parents about him yet. For one thing, she wasn't sure how they'd feel about the fact that he probably wasn't a member, since she hadn't seen him at church or seminary. For another thing, there was nothing to tell.

Besides, the fact that she had such a massive crush on a guy she'd barely exchanged twenty words with was embarrassing.

She didn't have to talk to him to know him, since she knew what his heart looked like. But if she told her mom that, she'd have to explain about the visions, which she preferred to keep private. And if she didn't explain about them, her mom would probably badger her for details that she didn't know and wouldn't want to pester Alex to get.

Better to just not talk about Alex right now.

They drove to her father's coworker's house, and Amanda's father rang the doorbell.

A man with sand-colored hair answered the door. "Isaac! Good to see you. And you must be Mira and Amanda."

"That's right," Amanda's mother said, shaking his hand.

Amanda nodded.

The man invited them in and introduced them to his wife, Tammy, who was an African-American woman with very short hair and enormous hoop earrings.

"Are you allergic to anything in cheese soufflé?" she asked. "I forgot to ask."

"No, that sounds great," Amanda's dad said.

"Caleb! Jessica!" Steven called up the stairs. "They're here!"

The Words Not Spoken

There was a stampede that sounded like it belonged to a lot more than two people as two dark-skinned teenagers thundered down the stairs. The guy jumped down the last five steps and landed in a crouch.

"First!" he crowed, standing up.

"Jumping is cheating!" his younger sister cried.

"Can you try not to run down the stairs?" Steven asked, looking exasperated.

"He started it!" the girl insisted.

"It's like they're determined to embarrass me," Tammy snorted, shaking her head. Her hoop earrings swung.

Amanda's mother chuckled. "I have a son who's nineteen and another who's twenty-one. Amanda's the only one of the three who isn't rambunctious. Don't worry, we're used to it."

"In college?" Tammy asked.

"Joseph is. Wallace is serving a mission in the Philippines. He's been there for a year now."

"Cool! He got to go somewhere interesting instead of college?" the teenage boy asked enthusiastically, wedging himself into the conversation. "Hey, Mom —"

His mother gave him a narrow-eyed look. "Caleb."

"Y'know —"

"You're going to college," she said flatly.

He made a face and rolled his eyes at the ceiling.

"Why don't we go start dinner?" Steven suggested, in a very polite and even tone.

"Beat you there!" the girl shouted, bolting out of the room.

"Not a chance!" Caleb shouted, chasing after her.

"If you break anything, you're dead meat!" Tammy called.

The rest of them followed those two to the kitchen, where they all sat down to eat.

Amanda said a quick prayer over the food in her head, since Steven's family didn't seem to pray before eating, and then she accepted a helping of cheese soufflé that Steven dished out for her. Tammy's recipe seemed to include a lot of garlic, which she wouldn't have expected, but it was pretty good.

After trying a bite of roasted asparagus, which was underdone and way too crunchy, Amanda looked up to drink her milk and was surprised to see Tammy quickly glancing away.

"So do you two work in the same department?" Amanda's mother asked Steven.

He nodded. "Yes, under Catherine."

"Is she a good boss?" Amanda's mom asked. "I've heard she can be quite strict."

Steven hesitated. "She's . . . got high standards."

"I've heard one of Dad's other coworkers call her She-Who-Will-Not-Be-Named," Caleb put in with a grin.

Tammy and Jessica laughed. Steven didn't.

"Catherine doesn't expect any more than our best work," he said seriously. "It's just that she won't accept any less, either. And she's interested in results, not busywork. She rewards efficiency by letting us go home early if we're done sooner than anticipated. Few bosses do such a thing."

"That's true," Amanda's father said thoughtfully. "I saw her tell Belinda she could go home an hour early yesterday."

"Exactly." Steven nodded. "She's not easy to work for, but she considers long-term morale more valuable to the company than short-term gains. Overall, I'd say that having access to the information that only she knows makes her a far more effective boss than most."

"'Information that only she knows'?" Amanda's father looked puzzled.

Steven smiled slightly. "I'll explain what I mean after dinner. It's relevant to the reason I invited you here."

Amanda's mom looked taken aback. "Didn't you just invite us here out of friendliness?"

Steven shook his head. "No, there's something we need to discuss. But it can wait until we're finished."

Amanda felt a pair of eyes burning holes in her skull. She whipped around to see Caleb staring at her.

What? she thought defensively.

He grinned at her and waved.

The Words Not Spoken

Oh. He's trying to flirt with me. Amanda was unimpressed. She supposed Caleb was nice-looking, but he didn't hold a candle to Alex. Caleb was much too loud and exuberant. She'd gotten enough of that with her older brothers. She didn't need to date a guy like that, too.

"We *would* like to get to know you, though," Tammy said, serving herself another helping of the too-crunchy asparagus. "So, how are you settling in? Is there anything you haven't been able to figure out where to find around town?"

"Oh!" Amanda's mom said. "Do you know the best place in the area to get quality custom framing done? Amanda's working on something that I imagine we'll want to get a really nice frame for when she's finished."

Amanda's face heated up. She hoped her mom wasn't going to start bragging about her again. It made her uncomfortable when people talked about her paintings to people who hadn't seen them. She thought they should stand on their own, not be described.

"Oh!" Tammy looked surprised. "I don't know anything about getting things framed. Caleb, you took an art class last year. Do you know anything?"

Caleb snorted. "I took art last year because you *made* me. Stupid subjective junk. The teacher kept telling us there was no wrong way to do things, and then he objected to my final project because he changed his mind and decided there was."

"You turned in a pile of garbage that took you ten minutes to assemble!" Tammy exclaimed.

"Yeah, and it was symbolic of my feelings about the class, which made it *art!*"

"He totally failed the class," Jessica said with relish.

"I proved the teacher wrong, which means I *beat* it," Caleb said with satisfaction.

"I was hoping an art class would help him learn to be more patient and empathetic," Tammy explained to Amanda's mother. "It didn't work so well."

Incredulity turned to sudden discomfort as Amanda sensed someone's eyes on her.

She looked up and caught Steven's gaze. He looked down at his meal and kept on chewing.

Then she felt more eyes on her. Her head whipped over to Jessica, the younger teenager who was watching her openly with a speculative look on her face.

Amanda's stomach clenched. *Okay, why does everyone keep staring at me? Why ME?*

After what felt like forever, the meal finally ended, and Steven got up and asked them all to follow him to the living room.

All four of the family members exchanged significant looks with each other as they did so, Amanda and her parents in tow.

Amanda's heart pounded. This was definitely more important than they were trying to let on.

Once they were settled onto couches or chairs, Steven went to a bookshelf and removed a stack of papers from a top shelf. He unfolded the taped-together papers across the coffee table in the middle of the room, revealing a pedigree chart.

"I have reason to believe that you and I are second-cousins, Mira," Steven said, looking at Amanda's mother.

"Oh, are we really?" she asked with interest, leaning forward. "You're right. That's me and Isaac and our kids . . . oh, but you've got the wrong name for my mother's father's father."

Steven coughed. "Yes, well . . . I'm sorry to tell you that, biologically speaking, I don't think I have."

Amanda's mother looked up, puzzled.

Steven looked rueful. "The name you see there is my great-grandfather, and we have good reason to believe he is yours, too. He was not, shall we say . . . the most faithful of men . . ."

"Understatement," Tammy and Caleb said simultaneously.

". . . and he liked having affairs with married women. Quite a lot of those affairs produced children that nobody knew were his. We keep discovering new branches of the family that we didn't know we were related to. It turns out you're one of them."

Amanda's mother started to speak, then stopped. She started again, then stopped. "How would you know that?" she asked, finally. "Has there been a DNA test?"

"No, but we can get one done if you want," Steven said. "We figured this out by looking through old family records."

"Thankfully," Caleb said sardonically, "my great-great-grandpa was responsible enough to keep a list of all his conquests, just in case his escapades caused problems with unknown heirs later. Which they have about six times now. Such a very responsible slimeball. I'm so glad we're all related to him."

"'Heirs'?" Amanda's mother asked, looking puzzled.

"Yes, what you do mean by —" Amanda stopped abruptly, startled. She didn't seem to be able to say the last word. She couldn't even mouth it.

Steven's family members exchanged significant looks.

"Do you want to tell them?" Tammy asked her son.

"Nah, you can do it."

"You have a curse!" Jessica said brightly, staring at Amanda. "It's called the Aquarius curse. That means your personality's gonna get changed against your will, and then you'll die!"

Chapter 4
The Monetary Value of Everything

Looking numbly at the dark-skinned girl who looked about thirteen years old, Amanda thought, *What?!*

"Dad has a curse, too," Jessica went on cheerfully. "His is the Sagittarius curse. They work the same way, and they both stink."

"What are you talking about?" Amanda's father demanded, looking confused and angry. "There's no such thing as curses!"

"Ask your daughter to say the word," Steven said.

"What word?" Amanda's dad demanded.

"'Curse,'" Tammy said, glancing over at Amanda.

All eyes turned to her.

Shrinking down in the intensity of all those gazes, Amanda tried to say, "Curse." The word wouldn't come out. Her mouth wouldn't even form the shapes of the word.

"We call it word restriction." Steven's eyes were sympathetic. "Certain words are taboo to all of us. Once you know what they mean in this context, you won't be able to say any of them for the rest of your life. We don't know why, only that it happens to all of us. Caleb, would you care to provide a list?"

The Monetary Value of Everything

"Magic, magical, heir, power, curse, cursed, zodiac, and all the names of the zodiacs," Caleb rattled off. "You might also have some extra restrictions, depending on your power. Dad can't say 'illusion,' for example, and Catherine can't say 'worth' or 'value.'"

Amanda's father got up. "This is nonsense," he snapped, holding out his hand to Amanda. "They're worse than your aunt Lisa who believes essential oils can cure everything. Let's go."

Amanda took his hand and got up, clinging to her father's certainty for reassurance. But her heart wouldn't stop pounding. She *hadn't* been able to say those words, and what was that about illusion? She saw illusions, didn't she?

"Come on," Amanda's father said, holding out his hand to his wife.

She got up, looking reluctant. "I'm sorry, Steven, Tammy," she said politely. "I really do love talking about genealogy. But my husband's a bit sensitive about pseudoscience. My sister has a new quack theory every week, you see —"

Steven waved his hands, and the room around them abruptly transformed into the interior of a medieval castle.

Amanda's hand slipped out of her father's. She started to hyperventilate.

She looked over at her parents. Her father's face was white as a sheet. Her mother seemed to have stopped breathing.

"It's not pseudoscience, and we're not crazy," Tammy said in a very calm tone. "It's magic. Amanda will have a power, too, and using it will put her life in danger. Now, if you want to know how to protect her so that she lives a little longer, sit down, and we'll tell you."

Amanda sat down shakily. "Please tell me," she whispered.

She heard her parents sit down behind her. Neither said a word more.

Tammy gave a brisk nod. "I'll start with the basics. We don't know when or how the zodiac curses started. We do know that they've been around for at least two centuries, and we know that there are twelve of them, one for each zodiac sign. They all work the same way, so they're probably connected somehow."

"How do they work?" Amanda's father's voice cracked.

"Each curse changes the personality of the one who has it to match what it considers to be the ideal example of the zodiac sign they were born under," Tammy said. "Once it completely succeeds, that cursed person dies. At that point, their closest living blood relative who was born under the same zodiac sign will receive the curse."

"And that's what happened to me?" Amanda whispered.

Steven nodded. "We thought it was my third cousin Myrtle, but when my great-uncle died and she didn't have it, we realized that it must have gone to someone more closely related that we didn't know existed, and we started doing frantic research through my great-grandfather's records, yet again, to look for yet another branch of the family we'd missed. At last, we found your family line and traced the birthdays until we found you. If we'd known you were the next in line earlier, we would have warned you beforehand so you could prepare. I'm sorry we didn't."

Amanda swallowed. "How long have I had it?"

"About six weeks," Steven said.

She'd been cursed for that long, and she hadn't known it? "Why didn't I notice when it happened?"

"You didn't know what to watch for," Tammy said gently. "Have you had any urges to act out of character recently? Even in small and subtle ways? That's usually the first thing people notice. Sometimes even before they figure out what their power is."

Puzzled, Amanda shook her head.

"Well, watch for that. The more you resist the personality changes, the longer you'll live. I'm sorry to say that the longest anyone has ever lived after receiving a curse was twenty years. The norm is five to ten. You might be able to make it to fifteen if you are very careful and watch your thoughts scrupulously."

Amanda's breath caught. Fifteen years? Fifteen years, at the longest? That was all the time she had left to live? And it might even be five?

That wasn't enough time. That wasn't nearly enough time. It could have been worse, but . . .

The Monetary Value of Everything

She'd always assumed she'd live until her seventies, at least. She'd have a bunch of kids and tons more grandkids. She'd have her husband with her the whole time, and they'd die of old age within a few years of each other.

She hadn't realized she was being naïve.

"Now, as for your power," Tammy said, "it might be wise to watch for that, too. It might be something obviously magical, or it might take the form of information only you have access to. Catherine, for instance, always knows the monetary value of everything."

"Catherine?" Amanda's father asked from behind her. "You don't mean . . .?"

"Yes, our boss," Steven said, nodding. "I asked her if she'd be willing to hire you so that your family would move into town, where Amanda would be safer. She snorted and said absolutely not at first, that she wasn't a charity, but then I showed her the pedigree chart. As soon as she looked at your name, she changed her mind. Apparently she could tell just from that that you'd be an asset to the company."

"She's the Leo," Tammy put in.

"And she's very good at keeping our department efficient and profitable," Steven added. "When it comes to monetary value, she's never wrong."

Amanda glanced back at her father. He seemed to be digesting the news. "So I could ask her to confirm what you've said?"

"Absolutely," Steven said. "Please do, in fact. She has about a dozen different charts she's made that may be helpful. I've known her most of my life, since we both grew up knowing what we'd have eventually. She thinks data analysis can solve any problem. I'm not sure if that will do any good in this case, but it can't hurt."

Amanda's mother spoke up. "You . . . said Amanda would be safer here. Is that true?"

"A little safer," Steven said. "She'll probably live about twenty percent longer. Those who move here generally do. Having a community of others who understand what we're going through seems to help us endure."

"And there are twelve people in town with a curse like this?" Amanda's mother asked.

Steven sighed. "No. Only six. Olivia lives in London, and the other five are lost. We don't know who has them. That's very unfortunate because a person who has the condition and doesn't know it tends to die twice as fast on average, because they don't know how to fight it or even that they should."

With that, the topic of conversation shifted fully away from an important overview and over to nitty-gritty details, which Amanda's parents seemed interested in and Amanda was not.

She knew exactly what her magical power was, and she had no intention of sharing that information with anybody, so she let them talk while she turned it on to look at the four people she had just met. Her power was always surprising her in interesting ways.

The bored-looking teenage girl slumped over the edge of the couch's armrest, looking like she wanted an excuse to leave the room, turned into a flamboyance of hot pink flamingos.

Two of the pink birds stood off to the side, one gobbling up food while another tried to steal it away. Those were her and her brother.

Six more were preening their white and pink feathers while squawking and honking at each other. Those were her friends.

One was missing half its feathers and looked like it had been sick, but was now recovering. That was her mother.

One was mortally wounded and could barely walk, but was still trying to pretend that it was just fine. That was her father.

Amanda turned her gaze over to Caleb, who was sitting next to his little sister. Since her power was on, she heard his voice excitedly describing the way the curses' word restriction censored detailed *descriptions* about powers, not just particular words, but what she saw was a field of endless vistas of exotic locales.

"That's true," Steven said. "I can't describe what mine does."

Steven was a stagnant pond that looked like it had grown over with slime, and now was clogged with pollution and garbage. Amanda was deeply shaken to realize that the man who seemed so placid looked at himself that way.

The Monetary Value of Everything

"Even though you can show it?" Amanda's mother asked.

"Even then," Steven's voice said wryly. The stagnant pond in place of him burbled silently. "Sometimes the limitations seem completely arbitrary. For instance, if you use the same euphemism in place of the same taboo word for long enough, the euphemism will become a taboo word to you, too."

"Yeah, and sometimes cursed people can say forbidden words by accident if they're in a different context," Caleb added. "I heard Dad say 'power outage' a few months ago."

"Oh, yeah? I heard him complain about the neighbor boy cursing too much last week," Jessica said gleefully. "He didn't even notice he'd said it till I pointed it out!"

"So it's context-sensitive," Amanda's father said thoughtfully. "It's not the words that are the problem, it's what they mean."

"Exactly," Tammy said. "Small children who are cursed don't get the word restriction in place until they understand the meaning of the syllables they're repeating."

"And then there are foreign languages," Steven said. "If you don't know what a word means, you can say it, even if it would be a forbidden word if you did."

"And then there are homophones," Tammy put in. "Steven can say 'air' just fine, meaning the stuff we breathe, even though he can't say 'heir,' a person who inherits a curse."

Amanda wasn't paying much attention. Their conversation wasn't very interesting. But the vision of Tammy was riveting. She was an ice palace with intricate carvings along every wall and elegant sculptures tucked in every corner. There was a bright sun beaming through the window that seemed ominously close to melting the sophisticated beauty, but for now, it was holding firm.

She didn't bother to glance back at her parents. She knew what they looked like already.

"Oh, good grief!" Tammy cried, startling Amanda out of her visions. "Steven, we forgot to have you turn off your power!"

"Oh, right!" The man showed a hint of hesitance and regret before he waved his hands, and the illusion of a European castle vanished from around them.

Tammy explained to Amanda, "The more you use your power, the more the curse will advance. So it's better if you don't use it. Once you figure out what yours is, keep that in mind."

Amanda's eyes widened. "O-oh!"

Did that mean she shouldn't be turning on the visions? But she loved them! Besides, how was she supposed to paint Alex's cityscape if she couldn't get the colors just right?

Maybe she could turn her power on to watch Alex. Just Alex. He was the most beautiful of all. That would be fine, wouldn't it?

"That reminds me," Steven said, retrieving a wallet from his pocket and pulling a slip of paper out of it. "I keep this with me to remind me what personality traits my condition will be trying to push me towards. Have a look."

He handed it to Amanda, who read it. It said:

Restless, impatient, loves travel and adventure, great sense of humor, highly curious, and hates lies.

"So I should avoid those, too?" Amanda asked, looking up.

"No." Steven shook his head. "These are yours." He pulled another slip of paper out of his wallet and passed it over.

It said:

Rational thinker. Knows their own mind. Loves surprises. Values honesty. High ideals. Creative, intelligent, often shy.

Amanda's mouth went dry.

"But that's . . . me," she whispered.

"No, that's who you *shouldn't* be," Steven corrected her. "Try to avoid all of those personality traits as much as possible."

"But that's *me!*" Amanda cried. "That's me! That's describing me! That's how I am right now!"

There was dead silence and a lot of looks were exchanged.

"Oh, dear," Tammy said, sighing heavily. "It's not a good thing to already be close to where the curse wants you to be."

"Why?" Amanda whispered. "What does that mean?"

"It means you'd either better try to change fast," Steven said, "or you'll probably be dead within a year."

Chapter 5

To Fall in Love

Greenfell High School's lunch bell rang, and Valerie casually slipped into the school and waltzed down the hallway within a crowd of students, hoping no authority figures would notice that she wasn't a student here. She'd brazen it out and pretend to be a new student if they did.

It'd been a few days since her last visit here. She'd spent that time finding a cheap apartment, cleaning out the atrocious back of her van, and driving around town to familiarize herself with all the roads and stores here.

She'd even bought groceries instead of fast food, for once. If she was going to stay for awhile, and she probably would, she could cook some of her favorite meals on a stove. Not being able to do that was the one disadvantage of always being on the road.

So she'd been a little too busy to continue her search, since she'd assumed it could wait. But now she had time, and it was time to find the third person at Greenfell.

Maybe it would be someone with answers.

Valerie inhaled through her nose.

With a good twenty hours of silence behind her, since she hadn't talked to anyone since yesterday afternoon, her range was nearly half a mile now, and she had no trouble picking out the odors of the three unnamed connections to her, all of which were also connected with each other.

Two of them were in the direction she had found Amanda and the boy student on her first visit, so she assumed those were the same people and turned in the opposite direction to find the third one.

Her nose soon led her to a teenage girl who was dumping an armload of books in her locker.

"Hi!" Valerie said as the girl turned around.

All the odors vanished.

"Hi!" The girl looked startled. "Hey, I don't know your name! Are you new here?"

"Yep, I just moved in. I'm Valerie." She held out her hand.

"I'm Lucy." Lucy shook her head. "Nice to meet you! Where are you from?"

"Nearby," Valerie said. "My dad just got transferred." It was Amanda's story, so it seemed as good an answer as any.

"Oh, cool!" Lucy said. "Where does he work?"

There was no chance she was going to answer that truthfully! "He's a corporate drone."

"Cool. My dad's in the army. Hey, have you got a place to sit for lunch?"

"Not yet," Valerie said hopefully.

"Do you want to sit with me and my friends?"

"That would be awesome!" Valerie beamed. "I don't know anyone here!"

"Okay, cool!" Lucy said, grinning. "You're lucky we've got extra space. Carrie broke up with her boyfriend yesterday."

"Oh, no, I'm sorry!" Valerie gasped.

"Ehh, don't be." Lucy rolled her eyes and waved her hand. "Her boyfriends never last all that long. Carrie's kind of fickle. Make that *very* fickle. I think her longest relationship so far has been five weeks."

To Fall in Love

They got to the cafeteria and pushed through the doors. Valerie followed Lucy to the lunch line, wishing she hadn't had to lose her range to start the conversation. She was dying to smell what Lucy's connections with her friends were.

"Which table is ours?" Valerie asked as they left the line, each carrying a tray of food.

"That one," Lucy said, pointing. "Looks like Natasia and Sean are already there."

The table held a couple who were obviously dating. The girl was sitting on the boy's lap and feeding him potato chips. She kissed him on the forehead and he kissed her back on the neck, despite his mouth being full of chips.

"Friends of yours?" Valerie asked.

"Yeah, have been for ages. They've been dating for I think three years now?"

Envy gnawed in Valerie's stomach. "They look sweet."

"They look like the definition of 'public display of affection,'" Lucy said, rolling her eyes. "I love 'em both, but they can't keep their lips off each other, seriously."

Well, naturally when they walked past those two to get to the other side of the table, Valerie couldn't resist dodging close to the couple and giving the air between them a sniff.

Natasia and Sean broke off and stared at her in puzzlement.

"What are you doing?" Natasia asked.

"Oh, sorry!" Valerie laughed sheepishly. "I was trying to figure out what kind of shampoo you're using. It — uh — it's got a nice fragrance."

It was really inconvenient to not be able to use the word *smell* sometimes.

"Oh, it's in a purple bottle and has lilacs on it," Natasia said. "I don't remember the name."

"It *does* smell good," Sean agreed, burying his nose in the top of Natasia's head. "Mmmm."

"Your hair smells good, too," she giggled.

And the two were at it again.

Lucy looked at Valerie and rolled her eyes silently.

Valerie sat down next to her, hiding the wistfulness she felt. She liked the mix of connections between those two. There was tons of physical attraction, even stronger emotional attraction, a strong dollop of friendship, and a few shared-secret connections, all common things in a healthy relationship.

Will I ever have that? she wondered. *So far I've never even gotten close . . .*

A very hot Hispanic guy sat down at the table on the other side of Lucy. "Hi, gorgeous," he said, giving her a quick kiss.

"Hi, cutie pie," Lucy said, giving him another.

"I take it that's your boyfriend?" Valerie asked.

"No, he's just some random guy I picked up off the street!" Lucy said brightly.

The guy laughed and held out his hand. "Hi, I'm Pablo. Who're you?"

"Valerie." She shook it. "Lucy's letting me eat with you guys today because I'm new at school and don't know anyone."

"She's nice that way." Pablo draped his arm around Lucy's shoulders. "What brought you here?"

"My dad's work," Valerie said vaguely. "How long have you two been dating?"

"We're almost at our first anniversary!" Lucy said proudly. "Isn't he amazing? He's the sweetest guy ever, and he's suuuuper gorgeous. I don't even look at other guys anymore, because Pablo's so adorable."

"I try not to look at guys, too," Pablo said with a grin.

"Oh! *You!*" Lucy smacked him in the arm.

He laughed and kissed her.

"Anniversary, huh? That's cool," Valerie said, trying not to show the serious envy gnawing at her gut. "What're you going to do to celebrate?"

"Probably fend off his relatives," Lucy said darkly.

"My mother," Pablo said, rolling his eyes, "bought *wedding decorations* that she wanted me to approve last week. Can you believe that? Her excuse was that they were on sale. My mom and aunts have no sense of boundaries."

Valerie was startled. "Are you engaged?"

"No!" Lucy exclaimed. "But they've been doing this ever since our, like, sixth date or something! They drive me insane!"

Pablo stroked her hand. "Thank you for tolerating them."

Lucy grinned. "I'd tolerate a lot more than that to have you, cutie pie. You know that."

"I do." His eyes filled with warmth and fondness. "I'm lucky I have you."

"I know!" Lucy giggled.

Valerie giggled, too, even though she was extremely jealous. She'd love to have relatives with such a wildly lacking sense of boundaries.

She'd love to have anyone who cared she existed at all.

Well, she was working on it.

"Sounds like the ideal boyfriend," Valerie teased. "Is there another one just like him, or should I try to steal him from you?"

"Whaddya think, Pablo?" Lucy asked with a grin. "Are you stealable?"

He snickered. "Nah, you're the only girl I have eyes for."

Valerie sighed. "Well, then I'd better settle for second-best. Guess I'll have to make do with the guy I'm dating."

"Boyfriend?" Lucy asked with interest.

"Well, first date," Valerie said. "On Saturday."

"Good luck!" Lucy crossed her fingers for her.

"Thanks," Valerie grinned. She pulled her wallet out of her pocket and dropped it on the floor behind them. She wanted to smell what their connections were. "Oops! Hang on a second!"

She leaned over behind them to get her wallet, and sniffed as her nose got close enough. It was none of her business, of course, but she'd never let that stop her before.

The first connections that drifted into her nose were the ones between her and Lucy. There was the unnamed connection, as before. There was also a tiny hint of friendship, which was a pleasant surprise. Most people didn't form friendship connections, even weak ones, that fast. It seemed Lucy made new friends as easily as she did.

Then she caught the scents between Lucy and Pablo. They were a similar mix of what she'd noticed from the other couple: friendship, mutual romantic love, physical attraction, emotional attraction, shared secrets, wait what was that?!

Valerie's eyes widened as she straightened up, wallet in hand. *That's the same unnamed smell that connects me and Lucy!*

Except it was just a tiny hint between Lucy and Pablo. And he had no connections to Valerie at all. Which made no sense if he had that connection with Lucy, and she had it with Valerie, and everyone else who had it was connected with each other!

Unless, of course, there were a ton of people in town with a hint of that connection with somebody, and she hadn't noticed it before because it was so subtle, while the strong ones were so obvious and all linked with her.

"Hi, Matilda! Hi, Jezza!" Lucy called, waving to two more friends of hers who were approaching the table.

Valerie breathed in deeply through her nose. She hadn't talked for several minutes, so her range was about six feet in all directions. That was enough to smell the connections between Lucy and the two girls who were sitting at the table across from them.

"This is Valerie," Lucy said, gesturing over at her. "She's new, so I said she could eat lunch with us today."

"Okay," one of the girls said.

"Sure," the other said. "I'm Jezza."

"Matilda."

"Valerie," Valerie said, breaking her range.

There was nothing surprising between those girls and Lucy. Only friendship, and a few shared secrets. No hint of that unnamed connection. The same thing was true of Lucy's connections with both Natasia and Sean.

But getting another whiff of the odors between Lucy and Pablo had confirmed it: that hint of the unnamed one was definitely part of their mingled aromas. It was mixed in with the romantic love and physical attraction connections, of all things.

What in the world?!

She hadn't been this baffled about a smell for years.

She'd been starting to wonder if it might be some variant of the blood family connection, even though it smelled more like shared-suffering, because they seemed to work the same way. Both were connections that didn't fade over time, could be present even if both parties were unaware they were there, and were equally strong between everyone who had them.

But this . . . this was just . . . weird.

Another friend of Lucy's arrived with a lunch tray, and Valerie cheerfully waved and shook her hand and chatted with the girl, who turned out to be the aforementioned Carrie.

If she kept on inviting herself to their table and pretending to be part of the group, she was sure real friendship connections would start to form, and that might be a good thing. It would be nice to be part of a group again.

But groups were far more fragile than what she was trying to build. Casual friendships were easily made and easily broken. Besides, if she kept showing up at school, someone would notice that she wasn't a student and she'd get in trouble.

Nah, it wasn't worth the bother to chase the group. But Lucy might be a friend worth getting to know better.

Especially if Lucy knew what the unnamed connection was.

Chapter 6

To Be Herself

With regret, Amanda pulled down the unfinished watercolor canvases from her bedroom walls that she had only just unpacked a few days ago. She had hung them up only a few hours before learning about the Aquarius curse. And now she had to take them down and put them away.

She'd spent days trying to come up with some other way to fight the curse, and she had kept returning to the same inescapable conclusion. She had to give up something.

Rational thinking, intelligence, high ideals, and honesty were all things she wasn't willing to give up. She couldn't just snap her fingers to overcome her shyness or prevent surprises, either.

But creativity *was* something she could gouge out of her life.

Pulling down the half-finished kittens, she brushed the canvas with her fingers. She'd never be able to paint the strands of fur now, the soft swish of final details that were the most satisfying part of any composition.

Removing the canvas of her favorite temple, she bit her lip, regretting that she had barely started it.

And she was *almost done* with the laughing baby, which she'd wanted to paint ever since she'd baby-sat for the Johnsons back home!

But worst of all were the ideas that she would never be able to paint. The cityscape, for example. It was a mental image she still ached to capture. She hadn't even been able to doodle it; whenever she'd tried, her mind had gone blank. She probably couldn't do it justice, but if she could just mix the colors . . .

Amanda's hand reached unconsciously for her box of paints, which she had left on the bed.

She stopped and drew her hand back. *No. No. No.*

If she wanted to live, something had to go.

Art had to go.

There was a lump in her throat as she rolled up her brushes in the cloth and tucked them into the box. Then she packed up her paints and put them in, too. The smaller canvases that would fit in the box, she piled on top.

Amanda's mother came into the room, watching her. "You don't have to do this, you know," she said quietly.

Amanda shook her head. "I don't have a choice."

"Yes, you do. If it's two or three years of being miserable or one year of being happy, I'd rather you be happy."

"It's not just my life. I have to protect Tina."

They'd worked out that her cousin Tina was most likely her heir. Even though the curse had come from her mother's side, it could move to someone in her father's family after she died, and it seemed it was going to.

They hadn't been sure at first whether it would be Tina or her younger sister Paula, since the two had almost the same birthday, so they'd called up Steven to ask. He'd told them that the heir would be the one who was closest in age to Amanda.

Amanda liked her cousin Tina. She didn't want to die and dump the curse on her.

Or, well, die at all.

Not that you could call spending the rest of her life without making art "living."

"But you love painting," her mother protested.

"I do. And Tina's future is my responsibility. The sooner I die, the sooner she gets what I have."

"It's okay to live for yourself sometimes, you know."

Amanda breathed in deeply and exhaled. It would be so easy to make that excuse and just succumb to the curse. The same thought had occurred to her. But she shouldn't.

"No, it's not," she said in a mostly level voice. "I looked it up. Selfishness is one of the traits I should be avoiding."

Her mother walked over and put a hand on her shoulder. "In that case, if selfishness is one of the traits of Aquarius, you're not like Aquarius at all."

Amanda gave her a brief smile. "Thanks, Mom."

She put the lid on top of the box and carried the box to her closet. Standing on top of a chair, she slid it onto the top shelf, all the way into a distant corner, where she wouldn't have to look at it and remember how badly she missed it too often.

"Have you figured out what your power is yet?" her mother asked.

Amanda bit her lip. "What's the point?"

"What's the *point* of figuring out your magical power?"

"Yes. It's better if I never use it. What's the point?"

"It might be something you'd like. It might be something that would bring joy to your life."

"Yes, that's what I'm afraid of." Amanda picked up the two remaining canvases, which were both too large to fit in the box, and stepped up on the chair to put them carefully on top of the box with the others.

At least she'd given away all of her finished paintings to her friends back home. She didn't have to hide them away now.

"Do you want to move back?" her mother asked quietly.

Amanda looked down at her in surprise. "Move back?"

"Yes. Do you want to go back to your friends and our family back home?"

Amanda took a deep breath. "No. It's better for us to stay. It might help me live a little longer."

"That's true."

"Besides, Dad getting such a great job is the only good thing that's come out of . . . this happening to me. I may not get the benefit of having an adult life without student loans, but Joseph and Wallace will."

"I'm sure they'd understand if you wanted to go back home instead."

"On top of that, if you and Dad continue to live here after I'm dead, you may be able to have Tina come and visit. That may help her."

"I'm not really worried about Tina right now."

"That's okay," Amanda said. "You don't have to be. I do."

Her mother went silent.

Amanda got down from the chair and moved it out to the hallway to take to the kitchen. She went back into her bedroom and looked around. The walls were so stark and empty. This room, which had been starting to feel like a new home, was now cold and lifeless again.

There was a lump in her throat.

"Amanda," her mother said, her voice strained, "if you find something here that will make you happy that isn't dangerous, please promise me that you'll go for it. I don't want you to give up everything that makes you yourself."

Amanda nodded. "I'll try," she said quietly.

～～～
～～～

There *was* something that made her happy at school, and that was sitting by Alex at lunch every day.

Neither of them usually talked much. It felt unnecessary.

She often looked up to sneak glances at him. Every so often she would look up and notice him glancing at her, and she'd feel a thrill all the way down to her toes.

He liked her too, right? Didn't he? Didn't he?

Sometimes she desperately wished he'd ask her out on a date. She was a little too chicken to ask him herself, even though she was pretty certain by now that he didn't have a girlfriend.

But . . . but, well . . . this was good, too. She liked sitting across from him and looking at him. She could wait patiently.

On Friday, the fifth day of their sitting together, Amanda patted her mouth with her napkin and started to get up.

"Hey," a quiet voice said from across the table.

Amanda's head shot up. "Yes?"

He looked like he was struggling to get up his nerve.

Oh, my gosh! Is he going to ask? Is he going to ask? Amanda's eyes widened, and she waited breathlessly.

"Um . . ." Alex looked down at the table. "Would you be . . . um . . . interested in meeting me at Brudger's Ice Cream Parlor after school today?"

"Yes!" Amanda exclaimed, and then stopped herself. She didn't want to scare him off by acting too excited. "I mean, yes. Definitely. I'll be there."

"Really?" Alex looked up, his eyes shining with hope.

Amanda beamed and nodded excitedly.

Alex's face split into a wide grin. "Well . . . then I will, too!"

The bell rang.

"Okay," Amanda said in a higher pitch than usual, her heart beating so fast that she could hardly hear herself speak. "Okay, well — I should — probably go to class!"

"Me, too!" Alex said, looking a little giddy.

Her last two classes of the day seemed to take a million years, especially since she kept having to stop herself from doodling his face on her notes. It was really, really hard to never let herself draw things.

But at last, the last bell rang, and she was free! She ran all the way to Brudger's Ice Cream Parlor. Unfortunately, that meant she got there first, which meant she had to wait, chewing her lips into a wreck nervously.

She sat in a booth by the door while other students arrived and got in the line for the cash register. Every time the bell tinkled at the door, she looked up, and it kept not being him.

Finally, after what felt like forever, she looked up, and a pair of identical Alexes walked in.

To Be Herself

Amanda's mouth opened in surprise. *Does he have a twin?*

It was impossible to tell them apart. If only there was some way —

Visions opened before her. On the right was the meticulous cityscape. On the left was a cyclone of chaos.

Amanda gasped, and the sights disappeared.

She got up and ran over.

"Hello, Alex," she said to the one on the right. "Who are you?" she added, looking at the other one.

His eyebrows rose. "You can tell us apart? I'm impressed."

"Me, too," Alex said with a warm smile.

"Well, you're different," Amanda said, glowing with pride.

She probably shouldn't have used her power, since using it would advance her curse, but she'd done it by accident, and anyway, Alex was gorgeous when she turned her power on.

Not that that was an excuse.

Wait, no, that was a terrific excuse.

Now she was dying to turn it back on again.

"Not as different as you might think," the stranger smirked.

The smile dropped from Alex's face. "Xander. Would you go home?"

"Almost," he said in a singsong voice, looking over at Amanda. "So, you like Alex, do you?"

Amanda's face heated up. "Ex-excuse me?"

Xander held out his hand. "I'm Xander. Pleased to meet you."

"Amanda," she said, accepting the offered hand and shaking it. "Pleased to — yeeeeeeeeeeek!"

She yanked her hand out of his grip as he tried to kiss it.

"Xander!" Alex snapped. "Go home!"

His twin doubled over in laughter. "Oh, man! That was great! I like you! Let me know if you decide you prefer me to him, hm?"

"Xander!"

"I'm going, I'm going." Xander grinned lazily and waved, then sauntered out of the building.

"Well, that was . . . something," Alex muttered, his face red. "I'm sorry. I should have guessed he would do that."

"Your brother?" Amanda asked.

"More like the pain in my neck. He probably flipped a coin to decide whether or not to follow me in here."

Amanda giggled. "Sounds like a protective brother."

Alex smiled slightly. "He's definitely one of those things."

By mutual, silent agreement, they went to stand in line for the cash register. Amanda glanced at the flavors in the freezer, enticed by several she'd never tried before, then remembered that it was probably better to avoid good surprises if it was possible, and finally decided to stick with her favorite, which was cookies and cream.

It was their turn at the cash register.

"Cookies and cream with fudge syrup," Amanda said.

"And french vanilla with graham cracker mix-ins for me," Alex told the cashier.

Then he paid for both of them without asking, which meant this was definitely, unambiguously a date.

Good! Good! Good!

Amanda couldn't stop grinning as she followed him over to the table and they sat down and started eating their ice cream. They resumed their usual pattern of eating in silence and looking at their food, except she thought he was looking up at her a little more often than usual, and she was looking up at him more often than usual, too . . .

She wanted to look at him through her power, since she was pretty sure she knew how it turned on now, and he was far more beautiful that way, but no no no she shouldn't do that. No using her power on purpose! Bad!

Maybe . . . maybe there was something else she could do, though. Something that wasn't so dangerous.

Amanda switched her spoon over to her left hand and moved her right hand to the middle of the table, fingers facing upwards. She left it there, glancing up every few seconds to see if Alex would notice it.

Would he know what she meant? Would he catch the hint? Would he see?

To Be Herself

Alex noticed her hand. He looked up at her. She smiled shyly and felt her face heat up.

His hand crept across the table and settled on top of hers.

She laced her fingers through his.

They kept on eating one-handedly, but now they both went much more slowly, making every spoonful last twice as long and scraping the bottoms of the bowls long past the point that the last traces were gone.

When it got to the point that it would be ridiculous for them to keep pretending there was still some scrap of ice cream to eat, Alex stood up without letting go of her hand, so Amanda stood without letting go of his.

They collected their plastic bowls and spoons and wrinkled napkins one-handedly and deposited them in the trash can. Then they left the ice cream parlor, fingers still laced together.

"Which way are you going?" Alex asked in his quiet voice.

"That way." Amanda pointed off to the left. "You?"

"That way." Alex pointed off to the right.

Nooooo! Amanda bit her lower lip.

"Do you want me to walk you home?" Alex asked.

"Yes!" Amanda said, brightening.

They walked at a strolling snail's pace, turning the half hour walk into an hour and a half, their fingers laced the whole way.

When at last they reached the door of the apartment she shared with her parents, Amanda reluctantly let go of his hand and unzipped her purse to fish out her key.

"Will I see you at school tomorrow?" Alex asked shyly.

"Yes!" Amanda exclaimed.

He smiled. It was like a flower blooming.

Amanda went into the apartment and closed her eyes. *Oh, I wish I could paint his face.*

And the cityscape that symbolized him. Either on its own or paired beside the cyclone that symbolized his brother. It would be striking to paint both images on the same canvas, juxtaposed next to each other. They were opposites, and yet the colors used were exactly the same.

But she couldn't. She couldn't, because giving up art was worth it to live longer if it meant she'd have more time with Alex.

He was a man worth living for.

~~~

Alex was writing in his journal an hour later. He was smiling so much that his face hurt.

She's sweet and gentle, and she doesn't feel the need to talk constantly, he wrote. *When she smiles, it's like the sunrise. When she's quiet, it's like music. I love her.*

He stopped. He looked back at the words he'd written. He read the last few again. And again. And again.

Oh, wow, he thought, swallowing. *Really?*

He couldn't feel that strongly about her after the first date, could he? And all the days they'd sat at lunch together. And all the hours apart from that when he'd kept thinking about her . . .

He couldn't feel that strongly after the first date. Could he?

Alex's hands were shaking too much to write, so he capped the pen and put it and the journal away. Then he sat back and closed his eyes to steady his nerves.

He wondered what Xander would think.
~~~

Chapter 7

A Place He Wants
to Visit

Caleb yawned as he headed down the hallway, stretching his stiff arms as he headed to the bathroom for his morning shower, when he suddenly became aware that he was surrounded by mummies.

Oh, no, Caleb thought with alarm.

He bolted through a wall of hieroglyphs that wasn't there, smacked into the door at the end that he couldn't see, and fumbled for the doorknob to his parents' bedroom several feet above where some kind of old vase appeared to be. Then he flung it open.

"Dad!" he shouted. "Wake up!"

"Huhh?" His father sat up, bleary-eyed. His hair was a mess.

"Mummies!" Caleb shouted. "In the hallway!"

"What're they doing there?" he murmured, yawning.

"Gee, I wonder," Caleb said sarcastically. "Were you dreaming about Egypt?"

His father looked around, taking in their inside-of-a-pyramid surroundings. "Oh, sorry," he said, yawning again, and the house returned to normal.

"What's going on?" Caleb's mother mumbled from beside him. She pulled off the sleep mask she wore.

"Dad," Caleb said with a barely restrained temper, "was using his power in his sleep again!"

"I don't mean to," his father said, leaning over to collect the container with his contact lenses from his bedside table. "It just happens."

"I know, dear." His wife kissed him.

Caleb was less patient. "If you keep doing that, you're gonna die sooner! You're supposed to live the full twenty years!"

"There's nothing 'full' about it, Caleb," his dad sighed, sliding his feet out from under the blankets and onto the throw carpet that covered the hard wood floor. "Twenty years is the maximum anyone's ever lived, not a guarantee. It's rare to get past fifteen."

"Well, *you're* going to live for twenty years," Caleb insisted, following his father down the hallway to the bathroom.

"That would certainly be nice," his dad said, reaching for his toothbrush and pulling it out of the holder. He rinsed it under the faucet and tapped it on the side of the sink.

"Which means fourteen years left," Caleb bulldozed on. "At *least*. You want to be alive to meet your grandkids, right? I'm not gonna have any for, like, ten years. And Jessica? It could be twenty! So you have to beat the odds and do better than anyone ever has before!"

His father squeezed toothpaste onto the bristles. "Yes, that would be nice, but I don't think you should count on it."

"Why not?!" Caleb demanded. "You can control it, can't you?"

"Some," his father said. "Not as much as I used to be able to. It gets harder to resist every year. That must be why the effects seem to accelerate with time. I'm starting to think the difficulty curve may be more exponential than linear."

That enraged Caleb. "Then fight it exponentially harder!"

"There are limits to human capacity."

"Dad, you always said you'd live for twenty years after getting the curse! You always said that was the whole point of making sure you didn't have any Sagittarius traits!"

A Place He Wants to Visit

"Yes, and now I'm telling you that I was overconfident, which means it's even more important that you prepare yourself in the same way," his father said. "You're way too close to where you shouldn't be already. Do you want to be in the same position as Amanda?"

"What, you mean having both her parents alive, and neither of them cursed? Sounds great!"

"Don't be difficult, Caleb."

"I wouldn't have to be difficult if you hadn't made me the Sagittarius heir *on purpose.*"

His father sighed. "Do we have to go through this again?"

"'A lost curse is an inherent evil,' yes, I know," Caleb said in a sarcastic tone. "And let's see, what's the other excuse you usually make? 'I wasn't going to curse somebody else's child if I wasn't willing to curse my own.'"

"I'm sorry you don't like it," his father said in an even voice. "We couldn't ask your input. It was going to be somebody, and we wanted to make sure it was someone who knew what was going on and how to fight it."

"*Jessica* didn't get born in the curse dates," Caleb grumbled, picking up his toothpaste and brushing his teeth while his dad did the same thing.

His father left the bathroom, so Caleb picked up his shampoo from the counter, about to get in the shower. Then his younger sister waltzed in.

"Hey!" he protested. "Ever hear of privacy?"

"Ever hear of shutting the door?" she retorted.

"I have a date to get ready for!"

"Oh, good, does that mean you'll be primping for an hour again?"

"*You're* the one who takes forever in the bathroom!"

"I timed you last time you were doing your hair. It was fifty-five minutes. You don't even have that much hair to style."

"Get out!"

She stuck her tongue out at him and left to go to the downstairs bathroom instead.

Caleb was done with his shower and had his hair styled right in only thirty-five minutes, *thanks very much,* and then he went to pick out his clothes.

He was ready to go and out the door only twelve minutes later. He'd be there ten minutes early. He was usually early to things he was excited about.

〜〜〜

Valerie was ten minutes late.

Caleb was standing and tapping his foot next to the crosswalk where they'd said they would meet, checking the time on his phone every two seconds and wondering if he should call her.

She arrived in a beat-up, clunky old van and parked at the parking lot of the strip mall beside him.

"Hi, Caleb!" she called as she jumped out of the driver's seat and shut the door. "Sorry I'm late! I ran into someone I've been wanting to get to know better, and we were swapping contact info."

"Was this a guy?" Caleb asked with a suspicious side-eye. He was trying not to act grouchy.

"No, a girl called Lucy," Valerie said, hurrying over. "She's a junior at Greenfell. You probably don't know her."

"No, I know her," Caleb said, barely suppressing rolling his eyes. She was the Virgo. He knew her quite well.

"Oh, really?" Valerie asked shrewdly. "Ex-girlfriend?"

Caleb barked out a laugh. "She wishes!"

"Is there a history there I should know about?"

"Not really," Caleb shrugged. He could hardly say, *She has a power to make guys fall for her, and she used it on me, and I acted like a pathetic wimp, and that was the most cringe-worthy afternoon of my life.* Valerie wouldn't believe any of that. Besides, it wouldn't make him look cool.

"Okay," Valerie said. "Have you had breakfast? If not, there's a breakfast buffet I found near the hiking spot that's really good. I'll pay. Unless you want to."

Caleb grinned, his annoyance at her tardiness evaporating. "I never object to free food."

A Place He Wants to Visit

"And you wore sneakers," Valerie noted, looking at his feet. "Good. Smart thinking."

"What else was I going to wear? High heels?"

Valerie guffawed. "Oh, man, now I'm imagining that!"

"You don't have to imagine it," Caleb said, thumbing through his phone. "I got dared to wear a pair of red high heels to school once. Lemme see if I can find the pictures."

He found them and pulled them up and flicked through them so she could see.

She almost fell over laughing. "You didn't tell me about the feather boa and the makeup!"

"It was on a *dare*," Caleb said, grinning. "Of course, then Jake had to come to school wearing nothing but swimming trunks, a snorkle, and an inner tube shaped like a rubber ducky."

Valerie howled. "Do you have pictures of *that?*"

"Sadly, no. He refused to pose for any."

"Aw, that spoilsport! When you get dared to do something ridiculous, you *own* it! You don't get all embarrassed and refuse to pose for pictures!"

"I know, right?!" Caleb exclaimed. "Oh, here's one of me blowing a kiss at the ceiling."

Valerie cracked up and doubled over again.

"Hey, can I see your travel photos?" Caleb asked, reaching the end of the ones from his dare.

"Sure. I've got loads. They're not as great as yours, though. Wanna look at them while we're in the car?"

"Yeah, that sounds cool!"

"Okay." Valerie pulled her phone out of her pocket and flicked through it for a minute. "There you go."

He followed her to the van, they put on their seat belts, and he flicked through the first of the pictures while she turned on the car. "Man, you've been everywhere!"

"Not everywhere," Valerie said, glancing over her shoulder as she backed out. "I've only covered about a third of the country so far. I haven't been in a hurry."

"I can see why," Caleb said, flicking through. "This looks fun."

"It is fun," Valerie said, glancing over at him with a smile. She put the car in "drive" and headed out of the parking lot. "Maybe you should take some friends and go on a trip around the country when summer vacation hits."

"Can't," Caleb said gloomily. "My dad would never allow it."

"Again with your dad," Valerie noted. "What's he got against traveling?"

Caleb hesitated. He thought about telling her the whole truth, but there was no chance she'd believe it. Besides, he didn't want to spend the whole day moping and whining about his problems. "It's a family thing," he said at last. "Doesn't matter. Tell me about *your* family. What're they like?"

"Well behind me," Valerie said. "Where they should be."

"That bad, huh?"

"Probably not as bad as you're thinking, but not great, either. It's a long story, and I'd rather not get into it."

"You have friends back home?"

"Nope," Valerie said, turning the van on to the entrance ramp to the freeway.

"Why not?"

"Because my parents were crooks, and everyone I knew found out about it when I was in high school. Like I said, I'd rather not go into detail. It'll just make me mad again, and I'm trying to forget about it."

"Fair enough," Caleb said. He went quiet, looking through more photos.

"Okay, okay!" Valerie burst out. "I'll tell you. My parents are Luis and Valentina Gutierrez."

Caleb stared at her blankly.

"Ever hear of Mountain Hill Securities?"

"It was a pyramid scheme, wasn't it? I have an aunt who lost money on it."

"Ponzi scheme, not pyramid scheme."

"What's the difference?"

"Similar, except it looks more legit. Much easier to sucker people in."

A Place He Wants to Visit

"Okay," Caleb said. "I take it your parents were in on it?"

"It was their company. They owned it." Valerie smiled grimly. "They were defrauding everyone I knew, including my grandparents, for most of my life. When it all collapsed and they got caught and thrown in prison, guess how many of my old friends wanted to be associated with me?"

Caleb swallowed. "None?"

"Bingo!" Valerie clapped her hands. "Yessiree, even my own grandparents hated me! I can't really say I blame them, since I'm the one who convinced them they should invest everything in the company, even though my parents told them not to. Shoulda been a red flag, in retrospect, but my parents had all kinds of convincing-sounding reasons. They were really good at lying."

That sounded worse than Caleb could possibly imagine. "I'm sorry," he said. "That sounds bad."

"Yeah, which is why I left it behind me." Valerie glanced at her driver's side mirror and changed lanes. "I'd rather you not tell anyone about that, by the way. I'm sick of having people judge me by what my parents did."

"I can see why," Caleb said. "I won't tell anyone."

He wondered if he ought to tell her about his dad and the curse. He had a niggling feeling he ought to, but if he did, that would probably be all they'd talk about, and he didn't want to think about the curse when he was finally doing something interesting.

Besides, what if she agreed with his dad and told him that he shouldn't be going off on an adventure because he was practically the ideal Sagittarius already?

Forget *that.* He wasn't interested in fighting the curse at all. He'd die whenever he died. If that meant he'd follow his dad in just a few months, whatever. It wasn't like it was going to happen for another fourteen years.

It *wouldn't.*

"Still want to be spending the day with me?" Valerie asked, glancing over at him.

"Duh!" Caleb said. "You're hot, and you didn't tell your parents it was okay to be crooks."

Valerie grinned. "Thanks. You're not so bad-looking yourself."

"What's with the back-handed compliment?!"

Valerie laughed. "Okay, you're very *good*-looking, and I've been looking forward to this date all week. Happy?"

"Happy. But I want to know where you found this water slide." Caleb turned the phone around to face her. "Where was that? That looks awesome!"

"Um, I don't remember. There have been so many places."

Caleb flicked through more pictures, green with envy. He wanted to live the life she was living.

Chapter 8

The Boss of Me

"Um," Alex said shyly at lunch about a week after their first date, and after several more times walking her home, "my mom wants to meet you. Would you be interested in coming to meet her this afternoon?"

"Oh!" Amanda's heart hammered. "Sure!"

She hadn't introduced him to her parents yet. She had told them about the nice boy who kept walking her home, and her mother had looked very pleased and relieved. The thought of meeting his parents already was a little scary. But she could hardly say *no*.

She was more than a little surprised, after school, to find out Alex drove a motorcycle.

"This is Sir Horse," he said, introducing her to it. "Sir Horse, this is Amanda."

Her lips twitched. "You call it 'Sir Horse'?"

His face was pink. "I know it's goofy, but . . ."

"No, it's cute. I like it."

"Are you okay with riding on it?" Alex asked. "I know it's not as safe as a car, but it's cheaper, and it's way more fun."

Amanda took a deep breath. It seemed her dates with Alex were going to contain a lot of good surprises. Oh, well. That was why she'd given up art. Because you couldn't always stop surprises from happening. "Sure," she said.

He collected a pair of identical helmets from a bag at the side of the motorcycle and handed one to her.

"You have two helmets. Do you drive a lot of girls home?" she joked.

"No." He looked embarrassed again. "I share it with Xander."

"Oh, that makes sense. I shared a car with both of my brothers before they went on their missions. Joseph took it when he came back home and went to college."

Truthfully, both her brothers had offered to let her keep it, but she'd insisted Joseph take it because he would need it more. Since she now knew that she wouldn't be living much longer, that had certainly proven to be true.

Wrapping her arms around Alex after she got on the motorcycle so that she could stay on was . . . wow, she hadn't gotten *this* close to him before! But this was okay. This was good.

Now she was wondering when he'd kiss her.

Alex was an excellent driver, and the terror of having no side of the car between her and the road was ameliorated after turning the first few corners. She found herself laughing as the wind blew her hair behind her.

It wasn't long before they reached the apartment building where his family lived, which was all the way on the other side of town. Alex parked the motorcycle and they both got off, removing their helmets.

"Was it fun?" Alex asked hopefully.

"It was fun," Amanda smiled, combing out her wind-tossed hair with her fingers and handing the helmet to him.

"Good." Alex beamed and stowed both helmets away.

"Hey, this is a long walk from where I live. How've you been getting home? Has Xander been picking you up?"

"No, I've been calling my mom to do it."

That . . . would explain why she was anxious to meet Amanda.

The Boss of Me

Amanda felt Alex take her hand, which came as naturally as breathing to both of them now, and he led her to the door of an apartment on the bottom floor. When he knocked, a middle-aged woman opened it.

"Alex!" she said, hugging her son. She released him. "And you must be Amanda."

"Hello," Amanda said, holding out her free hand awkwardly.

The woman shook it and smiled. "Don't worry, I'm not going to interrogate you. I just want to get to know you. I assume you're the reason he's been smiling all week."

"Mom!" Alex objected, blushing furiously.

"Come in," she said, moving out of the doorway. "I've got lemonade, if you'd like some."

"I try not to drink sugar," Amanda said. "It makes me jumpy."

"Then you're probably healthier than I am. Alex?"

"I'm good with lemonade."

She headed to the kitchen, and Alex and Amanda went to sit on the couch, still holding hands. His mom came out and handed a glass to Alex, who took it with his free hand.

"So," his mom said, sitting on the couch next to Alex, "tell me about yourself, Amanda."

"Um," she said. "I'm a senior in high school. I have two older brothers. I just moved into town." *And I'm cursed,* she thought, but didn't say, partly because she couldn't and partly because that wasn't something you said to make casual conversation.

"Do you have a favorite subject at school?" the woman asked.

"Art," Amanda said without thinking.

"Oh, really?" Alex looked interested now. "What kind of art do you do?"

"N-nothing," Amanda said quickly, her face heating up. "I — I — actually, I've given it up. I dropped the class last week."

"That's a shame," the woman said. "Why would you do that?"

Because I'm trying not to die of a curse!

"Because there are, um . . . more important things I can be doing."

"Alex writes poetry, you know," his mom said.

Amanda looked at him with interest. "You do?"

"He does."

His face was red. "It's terrible, and you're not showing her any!"

"It's not terrible," his mom stage-whispered.

"Mommm!"

Amanda caught a glimpse of the hallway. "Are those baby pictures?" she asked, craning her neck to look. She loved babies.

"Oh, yes," the woman said, getting up. "Come see! I have a bunch of great ones."

Sure enough, the wall was filled with framed pictures. Most were of a little boy with curly hair. Some had two.

"Is that your husband?" Amanda asked, pointing to a picture of the woman in a white dress standing beside a tuxedoed man.

"Yes. He died eighteen years ago."

Amanda gasped. "Oh no! I'm sorry."

"Me too, but it happened a long time ago. We get by."

"Dad died when I was two months old," Alex said. "I don't remember him."

"What was he like?" Amanda asked his mother.

"Well . . ." The woman had a curious smile. "He was a lot like Xander. Very sweet, very charming, and not the most reliable. He was always good to us, though."

"I guess Xander takes after him, then."

The woman sighed. "More than you know."

"What was his job?" Amanda asked curiously.

"I'm ashamed to say he was a professional gambler."

"*What?*" Amanda gaped at her.

"I *see* you take my view of the matter."

"That's a *terrible* job!"

"It was, but there was no stopping him. When we got married, he was a tax lawyer. He changed rapidly."

"I'm sorry," Amanda whispered. She would hate for the man she married to turn out to have been pretending about who he was all along. That sounded just as bad as the curse.

At least she didn't have to worry about that with Alex.

Her power showed her the truth.

"Which ones of these are of Alex, and which are of Xander?" Amanda asked, waving her hands around most of the rest of the framed pictures.

"Good question," the woman said. "It's impossible to tell them apart. Alex, do you know?"

"Hmmmm." Alex scrutinized the dusty pictures and pointed to one. "I'm pretty sure that one's Xander."

"You think so?" his mom asked.

"Yeah, there's a hint of a mischievous smile."

"You'd be the expert."

"Oh, so this is so *cute!*" Amanda squealed, pointing to a picture near the top of two identical babies sleeping in a crib side by side. They had identical swaddling blankets, and everything.

"That one is cute, but this one's my favorite," Alex's mom said, tapping the wall over to the left. Amanda looked over and saw a picture of identical toddlers wearing the same clothes. One of them was busy building a tower of blocks. The other was standing behind him with a toy hammer raised to smash it.

Amanda cracked up. "I bet I can tell which one was which!"

"Oh, don't be so sure," Alex's mom said with a sly look over in his direction. "They weren't so different back then."

Alex cleared his throat, looking embarrassed.

"One might say they almost thought the same way."

"Can we change the subject now?" Alex pleaded.

"Oh, sure, sure." His mom laughed and headed back out into the living room. Amanda followed, and so did Alex.

"Well, I don't know about you, but I like board games, and I think they make great icebreakers," Alex's mom said. "We've got loads of them. Shall we play one together?"

"You mean, like *Monopoly?*" Amanda asked.

Alex's mother laughed. "We don't own 'Monotony,' which is what we call it. I'm thinking *Century: Golem Edition*. The art's pretty, and the rules are simple to learn."

"Sure," Amanda said.

She and Alex sat next to each other on the floor on one side of the coffee table while his mom got the box and came back.

Alex explained the rules while his mom was shuffling the cards and laying them out in the middle of the table.

"We play this one a lot," he said. "It's one of our favorites. Fair warning — she's mean."

"Hey, no kibitzing!" his mom laughed.

Sure enough, when Amanda was only one turn away from buying the golem she was aiming for, Alex's mom swiped it first.

"Hey!" Amanda cried.

"This is why you've got to keep an eye on what gems your opponent has!" Alex's mom said gleefully.

"That's okay." Alex stuck his hand up the back of her shirt and rubbed her back. "You'll get the next one."

Amanda instantly stiffened.

Alex froze and quickly removed his hand from her shirt. There was an awkward silence.

"Alex, why don't you go tell Xander to get some groceries for me?" his mom suggested.

"Oh. Yes. Good idea." Alex looked relieved. He got up and went down the hallway, opening a bedroom door. He went in, shut the door, and came out a second later with his twin walking behind him. They were wearing identical clothes again.

"You're really into the whole dressing alike thing, aren't you?" Amanda commented.

"All the better to confuse people with," Xander drawled, and gave her a wink.

"Have you been home the whole time?" Amanda asked.

"Yeah, I've been here. I was trying not to disturb your date." Xander smirked. "Do you want me to be noisy? I'll be noisy."

"List's on the fridge," his mom said, pointing to the kitchen.

"Yeah, yeah, I know." Xander went and got it. "See ya when I'm back!" He blew a mock kiss at Amanda and departed with a flourish out the door. A minute later, there was a roar of the motorcycle engine, and he was gone.

"Why do you two always dress alike?" Amanda asked Alex.

He shrugged. "It's easier that way."

"Easier for whom?"

The Boss of Me

"Me, I guess."

"Who chooses the outfit?"

"Usually Xander, but we have about the same taste."

Amanda was amused. Her older brother Joseph had talked about what a bother it was to choose clothes in the morning, and griped that he wished they had uniforms at school. If she ever told him how Alex chose what he wore in the morning, Joseph would probably call it a brilliant system.

Alex's mom won, and they decided to start a new game.

Alex was shuffling the golem and merchant cards to place on the table when the door opened and Xander strolled in.

"Sorry for disturbing your date," he drawled. "I'd have waited outside, but the ice cream would melt."

"Ice cream? That wasn't on the list," his mom objected.

"It was on *sale*."

"We need to talk about budget," she said with annoyance.

"But it's your favorite flavorrrrrr!" He pulled a carton of mint chocolate chip out of the bag and waved it around tantalizingly.

She sighed and rolled her eyes. "All right, you're forgiven. Finish putting the groceries away and go to your room."

Xander put the groceries away, then strolled into the living room and plopped on the floor beside Amanda.

"I told you to go to your room!" his mother exclaimed.

"But I like this game. Besides, I want to sit next to Amanda." Xander grinned and scooted closer to her.

Amanda scooted away.

"Xander, go do your homework," his mother insisted.

"You're not the boss of me."

"Xander, go do your homework," Alex said quietly.

"Fiiiiiiine." Xander got up, rolled his eyes, and blew a kiss at Amanda. "See ya later."

After that, he did a pretty good job of staying quiet. There was one point where she heard a thump and then a muffled curse word from the bedroom, probably a textbook falling to the floor, and there was one point when Xander wandered out of the bedroom to go to the bathroom.

When he came out and saw Amanda looking at him, he waved at her saucily. But then he headed back to the bedroom and stayed out of the way again.

After the second game was over, Alex's mom got up and said, "Well, I think that's good. It was nice to meet you, Amanda. Alex, will you drive her home?"

"Of course," Alex said. He looked at Amanda. "If that's okay?"

"Of course it is," she smiled.

"Or I could drive her!" Xander called from the bedroom. "I know where it is!"

The smile dropped from Alex's face. "No!" he called. "Stay out of the way!"

"How does he know where I live?" Amanda whispered.

Alex sighed. "It's impossible to keep secrets from Xander."

In other words, he'd been in the car when their mom had gone to pick Alex up.

They drove home together on the motorcycle, and it was starting to feel a little more natural to have her arms around him like this. Maybe she should hug him goodbye at the door.

Well. Maybe if he made the first move.

He didn't. But he did walk her to the door with his hand in hers, and then they smiled at each other for a minute before she got out her key and went in.

She waved to her parents as she passed their room, where they were getting ready for bed, and dumped her backpack in the corner. She'd worry about her homework later. It wasn't like school mattered anymore. She had early morning seminary tomorrow, which did matter, so she really needed to get some sleep as soon as possible.

She brushed her teeth, turned off the overhead light, turned on the light of her bedside table, and got in bed. She got out her Book of Mormon and her Bible, because she was trying to cross-reference all the Isaiah chapters with the ones in 2 Nephi, and found her notebook and pen to write down anything interesting she noticed. It was a project she'd been working on for over a year. The comparisons were interesting.

But her mind just wasn't focusing on scriptures tonight. All she could think about was Alex. She absentmindedly started doodling in the margins of her notebook. First Alex, then the game they'd just played, and then she started to draw the cityscape —

Her pen froze.

Amanda jolted out of her daydream, startled. What was she thinking? She wasn't supposed to be drawing! Not even doodling!

Wait, but . . . wait. Why had her pen frozen like that?

Hesitantly, Amanda put the pen back to the paper and tried to draw the first line of the cityscape.

Her hand froze again. It wouldn't move. She tried to draw the same line as the start of something different, and her hand moved easily to make it.

Amanda dropped the pen, even more frightened than she had been about the word restriction.

I can't draw it, even if I want to?!

She dimly remembered Caleb mentioning that some cursed people wound up with extra restrictions because of their powers. Steven couldn't say the word "illusion," for instance.

Well, Amanda could say words like "see" or "sight" or "vision." She just couldn't describe any of the specifics of what her visions showed her. So she'd assumed that constraint didn't apply to her, and hadn't thought any more about it.

But it seemed she had an extra restriction, after all.

Amanda squeezed her eyes shut and clenched her fists. *So even if I hadn't given up art, the curse would have taken my ability to paint the visions from me?*

Her choosing on her own not to paint the visions was one thing. The curse forbidding it was another entirely.

This was far more upsetting than not being able to talk about a few things. Far more.

Talking was just talking. Art was *art.*

She had never hated her Aquarius curse more.

Chapter 9

To Automate Everything

"So, what's your favorite subject?" Valerie asked Caleb, waving her fork around with a lettuce leaf on it. "That's something I haven't asked yet."

They'd been going out pretty much every night for the past two weeks, and tonight he'd taken her to Dave's Pizza Buffet. He'd been planning to let her pay, like she had for their last three dates, but she'd ordered him to do it, telling him the one who asked the other out on the date had to pay for it.

That seemed like a fair rule to him, especially since he didn't usually ask girls out; they usually asked him out. And then they usually made him pay.

"Math," he said.

"Math? Really?"

"Yeah. Is that surprising?"

"Kinda," she said. "After all the hours you talked about sports and how much you missed them while we were out hiking, I assumed it was P.E."

"Nah, I like P.E., but math's much cooler."

To Automate Everything

"What makes it cool?" Valerie asked.

Caleb slapped his hands on the table, excited. "It's the way it's always right, you know? Either it's right, or you did it wrong. There's none of that subjective junk. No grey areas."

Valerie snickered. "I take it you're not fond of English class?"

"No! It's such a pain! The teacher's always like, 'Figure out what what this means,' and I'm like, 'Okay, it means this,' and she's like, 'No! You got it wrong!' and I'm like, 'Then just tell me what the stupid thing means!' Gaaaaaah!"

"Heh! But math's always right?"

"Exactly! It's all black and white. So easy to understand. And everything can be turned into math. It's useful for everything!"

"True," Valerie said thoughtfully. "I use math all the time. It's really important for making plans when you're on the road."

"There's nothing that math can't make better," Caleb said with satisfaction.

"How about kissing?" Valerie grinned, leaning forward.

He took a bite of his pizza. "I'm sure it can improve that, too."

For some reason, Valerie rolled her eyes.

"Okay, your turn to answer a question," Caleb said, pointing at the salad on her plate. "Why'd you get rabbit food?"

"'Cause I noticed I've gained ten pounds over the past three months." Valerie pinched her side and grimaced. "I never want to eat healthy during the times I'm not talking. I've gotta do something to regain my figure."

"It's a great figure right now," Caleb said with a grin.

Her eyes gleamed. "You think so?"

"Obviously!"

She grinned. "I'm glad to hear that."

"What was your favorite subject? I mean, when you were in school."

"Hmm." Valerie thought about it for a minute. "I didn't really have a favorite, but I loved the debate club."

"Were you good at it?"

"I was *great* at it! The adviser kept telling me I should go into sales."

"I bet you'd be good at that."

"I bet I would, too." Valerie grimaced. "But I'm not so sure I want to anymore. My parents were really good at sales, too."

"Oh," Caleb said. "Yeah."

He got that. He didn't want to be like his dad, either. That was why he wasn't going to fight the curse.

"Hey, do you have a job?" he asked curiously. "How're you paying for travel in the first place?"

"Trust fund," Valerie said. "My parents' assets got confiscated, but mine didn't. I'm living as cheaply as possible so it'll last as long as possible. Technically it was *supposed* to pay for college, but that wasn't written in the rules, so . . . ." She shrugged. "Who cares?"

"What're you gonna do when it runs out?"

"Probably find a well-paying job with a high turnover and do that for a few months until I have enough to pay for my next year on the road." Valerie wrinkled her nose. "Not really looking forward to that when it happens."

"You could probably do a sales job on the road."

"I probably could, but I'm afraid of the kind of person that would make me. I have a feeling I'd start looking at everyone I met as a target to sell things to. That's what my parents did, y'know? I don't want to be a scumbag, even if it's legal."

Caleb grinned.

"What're you smiling about?"

"Just thinking you're really cool."

"Oh, really?" Valerie asked with a flirtatious smile. "How cool is that?"

"Very cool."

"Oh! Well, then!" Valerie got up and flopped next to him. "Why don't you tell me that in some other way besides words?"

"Okay," he said, holding up his hand. "Gimme five!"

She did so, looking really annoyed.

An alarm went off on Caleb's phone.

"Argh!" he groaned, checking it. "Mom said I had to be home early tonight because it's my turn to do the dishes."

"Do we still have time before I have to drive you home?"

"Ten minutes. We'd better eat fast."

Valerie groaned and went back to her seat, and they gobbled down the rest of their food quickly.

"Hey," she said as they were going out to her car, "when do you want to get together tomorrow?"

"That depends." He grinned. "Am I asking or are you asking? Just wondering from the perspective of who has to pay."

She smacked him in the shoulder. "If you're gonna be a brat about it, we could take turns."

"I'm cool with that," he said. "Or, I mean, we don't *have* to do stuff that costs money."

"Oh, really?" she asked teasingly, raising her eyebrows.

"Yeah, we can just walk around and talk. That's fun, too."

"Of course," she said, looking exasperated.

"Just thinking, if you're trying to save money, that would make sense."

"Well, I do like *talking* to you . . ." Valerie said, putting an odd emphasis on one of the words.

"Yeah, me too!"

Valerie sighed and shook her head as they got into the van for her to drive him home.

〰〰
〰〰

Caleb shut the door, waved goodbye, and headed straight to the front door of his family's house.

Valerie drummed her fingers on the steering wheel.

Caleb, she reflected, was definitely the densest guy she'd ever dated. How could he miss *every single signal* that she wanted him to kiss her?

She knew he *liked* her. In fact, not only were the physical and emotional attraction between them about ten times higher than on their first date, they were up to a full mutual-crush connection now. So why? Why was he so absolutely clueless? Why?

Did she have to tell him straight out? Was that what she needed to do?

But she didn't want to! She wanted him to figure it out!

Valerie grumbled under her breath as she turned the key in the ignition and backed out of the driveway.

Now would be the perfect time to have a female friend to talk to and dissect the guy's behavior. But she didn't have any of those here.

Or, wait . . . did she?

Valerie pulled over to the side of the road and found Lucy's number. She dialed.

"Hello, person on my phone!" said Lucy cheerfully.

"Hi, Lucy! It's Valerie. You remember me, right?"

"Duh! What's up?"

"Well, I just went out on a date with a guy who seems to be the densest person in existence, and I'm wondering if you can help me figure out what his deal is."

Lucy burst into giggles. "Sounds like fun! I'm baby-sitting right now, though. Actually, why don't you just come over here? Ellen's parents don't mind when my boyfriend drops by while I'm baby-sitting, so I can't see why they'd mind you being here. As long as you help me keep an eye on Ellen."

"Little kid?" Valerie asked trepidatiously.

"She's eight."

"Just the one kid? No, like, babies or anything?"

"Yeah. She's a nice kid. You'll like her."

"Nnnnn . . . okay," Valerie said reluctantly. Kids freaked her out. She never knew what you were supposed to do with them. "What's the address?"

Lucy told her, and as soon as Valerie hung up, she found the directions on her phone and drove there. She loped up the stairs and knocked on the door.

Hang on, Valerie thought, her eyes narrowed, looking around. *I think I've been here before . . .*

Nobody answered the door. She stood there waiting for awhile. Finally, she called Lucy back.

"Hey, Lucy, I'm here. I knocked. No one answered. Am I at the wrong house?"

"Oh, we're in the back yard! I must not have heard. Come around back."

Valerie hung up, went around back, and found a chain link fence with a gate. She pushed the gate open and saw a little girl swinging back and forth on a squeaky swing set.

I knew it! Valerie wanted to shout.

She had now tracked down six of the seven people with the unnamed connection to her, and that kid was one of them. She'd driven here last week looking for the one in this area. Since she'd found it was a kid, and she had no clue what to do with kids, she'd just driven on.

The other two people she'd found were middle-aged adults working at some sort of office building. Neither of them had looked particularly likely to hold a conversation with a random stranger, so she'd driven on from there, too.

It couldn't be a coincidence that Lucy was here baby-sitting this kid. Maybe that meant she really *did* know what the unnamed connection was.

Unfortunately, Valerie had kind of burned her ability to ask Lucy for details about what was going on when she'd introduced herself under false pretenses. She really should have thought about that before doing it.

Lucy was still under the impression that they were students at the same school. When she found out Valerie had lied, she probably wouldn't be willing to get overly chummy and confide secrets in her.

Oh, well, Valerie thought, pushing away her regret. It was too late to do anything about that now. *The unnamed connection is interesting, but the ones I'm building with Caleb are lots more important. It's great what a perfect match we are.*

Except for the fact that he was dense beyond all reason.

Maybe Lucy could help her with that.

"Hi, Lucy!" Valerie called, striding towards the patio where her new friend was sitting and playing a game on her phone.

"Hi, Valerie!" Lucy called, waving. "Ellen, this is my friend Valerie!"

"Hiiiiiiii!" the girl called. "Wanna see how high I can go?"

"Sure?" Valerie said.

The little girl with shoulder-length hair pumped her arms and legs faster to take the swing higher and higher.

"So tell me about this date," Lucy said, patting the patio chair next to her.

Valerie came over and flopped down. "His name's Caleb. I think he knows you."

Lucy sputtered a laugh. "Oh, if it's the Caleb I'm thinking of, yep, he *is* dense. Ellen, not that high!"

"But I'm Supergirl!"

"Be Supergirl a little closer to the ground! Okay, what's the problem with him this time?"

"He doesn't seem to notice that I want him to kiss me," Valerie grumbled.

Lucy smirked. "That's it? Well, that's a lot better than what he did to my friend Carrie."

"Oh?" Valerie asked with avid interest. "What'd he do?"

"Well, Carrie and I were on a double-date together," Lucy said. "Caleb was her date. And while she went to get food, he asked *me* out."

Valerie's jaw dropped. "No!"

"Yes," Lucy said emphatically. "And it gets worse. When I told him I wasn't going to date him as long as he was dating Carrie, do you know what he did?"

"What?" Valerie asked breathlessly.

"He said, 'Okay, I'll break up with her right now,' and went to *do* it!"

"No way!" Valerie burst out laughing. "That jerk!"

"I know! What kind of guy does that?!"

"Clearly a guy who wasn't that into Carrie in the first place!" Valerie cracked up.

"Well, to be fair, it was their first date," Lucy said. "But still!"

"Yeah. Still!" Valerie couldn't stop snickering. She could easily picture Caleb having done that, and it was such a jerk move. She was going to have to give him a hard time about that later.

To Automate Everything

"Ellen!" Lucy cried in alarm, standing up from her chair. "Stop that right now!"

Valerie looked over, startled. The little girl was still swinging, the swing creaking rapidly back and forth. The only thing that was different was that she wasn't pumping her arms or kicking her legs now.

What exactly was the problem?

Lucy stormed over and hissed in a voice she probably thought Valerie couldn't hear, "Don't be a lazy bum! You're not supposed to automate things!"

"But I'm tired, and I like swinging!" the girl complained.

"Do you want the you-know-what to get you? Because it's gonna if you keep using your thingy!"

Well, that was enlightening.

"If you're tired, you can go play in the sandbox," Lucy said.

"I just wanna keep swinging," the girl said in a sulky voice.

"Fine, you can stay on the swing, but if I catch you using your whatchamacallit again, we're going inside."

"I wooooooon't," the little girl muttered.

"So, what's this 'whatchamacallit'?" Valerie asked with great interest as Lucy returned.

"Nothing," Lucy said, waving her hand. "It's just a thing her parents want me to watch out for. That's why they have me baby-sit for her instead of other people."

"Oh, right, okay," Valerie said, significantly less enlightened and significantly more curious.

She wished she had a decent range so she could smell if there was a shared-secret connection between Lucy and Ellen. She was betting there was.

"So," Lucy said, plopping back in her seat, "what were we saying?"

"Caleb's the densest guy in existence."

"Right. Yeah, he is."

"Can you help me figure out *why*?"

"Do you really like Caleb that much?" Lucy asked curiously. "I mean, I think he's a jerk."

"Nah, he's not, he's just sure of himself, whether or not he should be." Valerie grinned. "I like confidence. It's sexy."

"Well, if you like him that much, and he can't get the hint, why don't you just tell him that you want him to kiss you?" Lucy suggested.

"But I don't wanna," Valerie complained, slouching back in her chair. "I want him to notice."

"Do you want him to notice, or do you want him to kiss you?"

"Ugh!" Valerie groaned, tilting her head back. "Yeah, okay, point taken. Fine, I'll bring it up with the clueless one."

"There we go. Problem solved. Saying things straight out is usually the answer with guys." Lucy glanced over at the swingset and did a double-take. "Ellen! I told you not to do that! Get off the swing right now!"

Valerie's head whipped over, and she saw the little girl hop off the swing. It kept on going without her, back and forth, exactly the same, with no loss of momentum.

Valerie's mouth opened slightly. *Whoa. That shouldn't be possible. What's causing that?*

Lucy ran over and caught the swing, and it stopped.

"Inside!" she ordered in a bossy tone.

The little girl stamped her foot. "But I was having fun!"

"Inside, or I'll tell your parents what you were doing!"

"You never let me have any fun!" the little girl shouted, and stormed up to the patio. She opened a screen door, marched through it, and slammed it shut.

"Sorry, Ellen's being a brat today," Lucy said. "I think I'd better send you home. Do you have your solution?"

"Probably," Valerie grumbled. "It just isn't the one I wanted."

Lucy laughed. "Really, Valerie, you've gotta work *with* a guy's weaknesses, not against them. If you like him, and he's dense, work around that, not against it. It'll end up better that way."

"Oh, thank you, wise guru," Valerie intoned, bowing.

Lucy put a hand to her chest. "I speak with the wisdom of one who has been in a relationship for over a year!" she said in a dramatic voice.

"Ah, the wisdom of the ages!" Valerie gasped, putting her hands to her mouth.

"Actually, I'm quoting my mom," Lucy said with a grin. "I'd better go check on Ellen now and make sure she isn't automa— um, getting into trouble again. Call me later and tell me how it went, 'kay?"

"'Kay," Valerie said, waving and heading off.

Her interest in what that unnamed connection meant had definitely skyrocketed. She was beginning to wonder if it might be something like "has-magical-power."

Chapter 10

The Pain in His Neck

Brushing her hair in the bathroom before going to bed, Amanda paused as she looked at herself in the mirror.

Can I see myself with my power?

Her stomach knotted and throat tightened.

No, no. That would be a bad idea. I shouldn't be using it in the first place. There's nothing to be gained by looking.

But it might tell her how close she was to the Aquarius curse. It might give her an idea of how much longer she had left to live.

Slowly, Amanda set down the hairbrush. She swallowed, looked at the mirror, and turned on her power.

The image of herself vanished, and instead, she saw a gallery with a tile ceiling that formed her favorite picture of Christ, and numerous paintings on display across all the walls.

All of them were people.

What? Amanda thought, astonished. *Does it work differently because I hold the power?*

No, her power told her. This was what Amanda looked like. She defined herself by the people she loved.

The Pain in His Neck

In the center were four large paintings on prominent display. She recognized two of them immediately. She had looked at her parents through her power before.

The first was of a farmer on a tractor, surrounded by open air and bright sky. Amanda hadn't realized until she'd seen this vision of his heart how much her father loved the outdoors and wished he could be spending his time there, rather than working in an office building.

The second painting showed a mama kangaroo, bending over to drink from a peaceful stream that trickled along over a number of slick rocks. She had three joeys with her. Two had left her pouch, and the third was poised to jump out.

Behind those paintings were two more that Amanda had never seen before, but she knew who those were immediately.

One of them showed two deer in a clearing in a forest in early spring. A young buck was trying to impress a doe with his magnificent antlers.

She *had* heard that her brother Joseph had a girlfriend.

The other showed a well-lit room with dozens of bookshelves crammed with thousands of books, each one a new subject that was begging to be learned. Lying in a recliner with fuzzy-slippered feet warmed against a cozy fire was Wallace, flipping through the pages of his scriptures. That was weird, because she'd never seen a non-metaphorical representation of a person in their own heart before. She wondered if it had to do with Wallace's massive ego.

Yep, her power told her.

Okay, so being on a mission hadn't taught him humility.

Amanda glanced off to the left and saw a wall of smaller paintings, all of them friends or relatives she'd left behind when they'd moved. The one in the center was Tina, the cousin whose life Amanda was responsible for.

Her painting changed more rapidly than the rest. It started out showing a Victorian woman with a parasol traipsing along a garden path. Then she stepped through an archway and became a rock singer at a concert. Then the singer spun around and was a ballerina, performing en pointe on stage.

That lasted for only a few seconds before the ballerina threw her head back, grew fangs, and became a pale-faced vampire in a spidery black gown that looked like it had come from a Gothic novel.

Amanda chuckled. That was Tina, all right. The two of them had little in common, but they had always appreciated the other's fondness for art. Tina loved fashion, and was always doodling it. She had even designed and sewn most of the costumes last year for the school play.

Tina would probably live longer under the Aquarius curse than Amanda had a chance to, but Amanda would try to keep her safe for as long as possible.

Then Amanda looked to the right.

Her breath caught.

There was only one painting there. It was Alex, on an easel, lit up by a spotlight. Some of his buildings were subtly different from the last time she'd looked, having a few details added or rough spots smoothed away.

Behind him was a wall of framed blank canvases.

Blank, because no one had been born to fill them yet.

Amanda gasped and turned off her power. Her face was hot, so she hastily turned on the bathroom sink and splashed water on her face, trying to calm her racing heart.

She shouldn't have looked. She shouldn't have looked. She shouldn't have looked.

She knew there were things she couldn't hope for. Things she couldn't want. Because the curse would take them away before she could live that long.

～～
～～

The next morning was Saturday, and Amanda needed more bathroom supplies, so she went with her parents to go grocery shopping.

"Oh! Add crackers to it," Amanda's mom was saying, looking over her husband's shoulder at the grocery list they'd brought. "I keep meaning to get more. We ran out."

"Any particular kind of crackers?"

"The good ones! You know, the ones with the things . . ."

"I think you'd better be the one to find them," he said dryly.

"Alex!" Amanda cried, seeing a head of familiar wavy hair stocking eggs in the dairy department ahead of them. She ran over. "I didn't know you worked here!"

"Amanda!" Alex looked up, startled. He tugged his employee vest self-consciously. "Yeah, I work here on Saturday mornings. It's how I keep Sir Horse in gas."

"Ahhhh!" Amanda's mother said from behind them. Amanda glanced back to see her smile and nod knowingly. "This is him, isn't it?"

"Who?" Amanda's father asked.

"The one who's been walking her home."

"Ohhhh!"

"Uh. Yeah. It's him." Amanda chewed on her upper lip. "Alex, these are my parents."

"Pleased to meet you," Alex said in a formal tone, bowing his head. "Thank you for allowing me the privilege of spending time with your daughter."

"Ooh, I like him," Amanda's mom said, turning to her husband. "I think this one's a keeper. What do you think, Amanda?"

Amanda's face heated up.

"You seem a nice young man. You can call me Isaac," Amanda's dad said, holding out his hand.

Alex shook it.

"And I'm Mira," Amanda's mother added.

"Uh," Alex said, looking awkward, "okay, Isaac and Mira."

"So tell me about yourself," Amanda's dad said. "You said you have a horse?"

"Uh . . . no." Alex looked embarrassed. "That's what I call my motorcycle. Sir Horse."

"Why do you call it that?" Amanda's mom asked.

Alex's face turned pink. "'Cause I pretend I'm a knight and Sir Horse is my horse?"

Amanda giggled. He was so adorable.

"I like a young man with a strong work ethic," Amanda's dad said with approval. "Are you able to keep your grades up?"

"Um . . . B minus average," Alex said with embarrassment.

"That's not bad."

"I could definitely do better, but . . . I kind of want to live my life and not spend all of it studying."

"That makes sense, too." Amanda's father nodded. "Do you play any sports?"

"I'm on the basketball team."

"Are you any good?"

"I'm not one of the best players, but I'm okay."

"That was me with baseball in high school," Amanda's dad nodded. "Granted, I mostly only played for the exercise."

"I like it," Alex shrugged. "I'm just not amazing at it."

"You'd rather be jousting, right?" Amanda's mother teased.

"Um . . ." Alex laughed sheepishly. "Yeah, if the school offered that as a sport, I'd be all over it."

"What are you thinking you'll major in?" her father asked.

"Honestly . . . I don't think I'm planning to go to college."

Amanda's father looked faintly disapproving. "You should go. You ought to be considering what you want to do career-wise. Unless you want to be stocking shelves for the rest of your life."

"College is expensive," Alex said. "We don't have the money, and I don't have the grades for a scholarship."

"There's such a thing as student loans."

"I don't want to rack up loads of debt, either."

"You really ought to be planning for the future," Amanda's father scolded.

"Isaac," his wife whispered, elbowing him, "that hardly matters right now, don't you think?"

"It does matter!" he insisted. "A young man should be thinking about how he can support a family —"

"Isaac!" she hissed, looking meaningfully over at Amanda.

Her father looked over at her. "Ah. Right. Yes. Good point."

Amanda tried not to cringe. As if she'd needed a reminder that she wasn't long for this world.

The Pain in His Neck

"All right," Amanda's father said, patting Alex on the shoulder. "Just keep making Amanda happy. Okay?"

Alex's cheeks flushed. "I'll try. Thank you."

"Well, we should probably let you get back to your job," Amanda's mom said. "Do you know which way we can find the crackers?"

"Aisle two," Alex said, pointing.

"Thank you. Very nice to meet you, Alex."

"Nice to meet you both, too."

They headed to the cracker aisle. As they turned in to it, Amanda's mom said, "Is he a member?"

Amanda shook her head.

Her mom sighed. "Shame. You should tell the missionaries to visit him."

"Mom!" Amanda blushed furiously.

"I mean, if he joins the church, he could take you to the temple —"

"I'm not really worried about getting married right now!" Amanda hissed.

Which was not true, because she was totally head over heels in love with Alex, but if she admitted that, she'd have to face the fact that she would never be able to have any of the things she wanted from life, and that hurt.

Now she wanted to look at Alex again.

"Hang on a second. You go on without me," Amanda told her parents. "I'll be right back!"

She ran to the end of the aisle and turned on her power. She wanted to check if Alex's cityscape that she'd seen in the mirror last night had been an accurate update.

When she looked where Alex was standing, she saw a cyclone of chaos.

No buildings, just a whole lot of rocks and wind.

Amanda froze. *Why, that little . . .!*

She ran back to the dairy department, where the employee was still stocking the shelves.

"You're not Alex!" she accused. "You're *Xander!*"

He turned around with a grin on his lips. "Hey, you noticed. Most people can't tell the difference. Well done."

"Why does your name tag say 'Alex'?!" she demanded.

"I can put whatever I want there. They don't care."

"You tricked my parents!" she said indignantly.

"You called me Alex," he said with a mischievous gleam in his eyes. "I think we're even."

She put her hands on her hips.

"Hey." Xander set down the egg cartons and sidled over. "After my shift's done, do you wanna hang out together?"

"No!" Amanda shot back. "I belong to Alex, not you!"

Xander's eyebrows rose. "You *belong* to Alex?"

Her face heated up. "Yes, I do. I'm his girlfriend, not yours."

"Oh, you're his girlfriend, huh?" Xander was grinning. "I wasn't aware that you'd had that discussion."

"Well, I *am!* So quit hitting on me!"

"Oh, I'm not promising that. There's no way I'm stopping."

Amanda spun on her heel and stomped away.

When she glanced back over her shoulder a second later, she saw Xander grinning up a storm as he watched her leave.

≈

"Your brother," Amanda announced as she sat next to Alex at lunch on Monday, "is a pain in the neck."

Alex looked sheepish, his shoulders hunched. "Uh . . . yeah, sorry about Saturday. Xander likes to pretend to be me."

"Why?" Amanda asked, baffled.

"Because he likes me better."

"Than . . . himself?" Amanda asked slowly.

"Yeah. It's a little complicated, but . . . yeah."

Amanda was silent for a long moment.

"That's sad," she said softly.

"It is," Alex said. "But it's better this way. Believe me."

Amanda looked up at him, querying.

He shrugged and didn't say anything. He just took a bite of his sandwich.

The Pain in His Neck

She picked up her slice of pizza and started eating it.

They sat in companionable silence for awhile.

Then she thought, *Hey, I should probably check,* and turned on her power. She looked over at Alex —

"It's *you!*" she shouted, jumping up off the bench. "It's you *again!*"

Xander nearly fell off the bench laughing.

"*You . . .! You . . .!*" Amanda shook her finger.

"Just testing you," Xander said with a gleam in his eyes. "I'm impressed you could tell. I'll go get Alex."

Amanda responded with an incoherent snarl.

Xander waltzed out of the cafeteria and came back a few minutes later with Alex in tow. He dumped him on the bench.

"She's all yo-uuuuuuurs," Xander said in a singsong voice. "Because she *belongs* to you. By the way, did you know she's your girlfriend?"

Amanda put her face in her hands.

Xander sauntered out of the cafeteria.

Amanda recovered, removed her face from her hands, and turned on her power. She looked directly at Alex.

She saw the line of buildings she'd been wanting to see. They were, indeed, updated in the way she'd seen in the mirror, with a few more tiny changes. The sun had risen slightly, and the light was brighter. That had never happened before.

When she turned off her power, his eyes held a mix of fear and joy that she couldn't explain.

Let's try this again, she thought, taking a deep breath.

"Your brother," she said, "is a pain in the neck."

Alex said softly, "I'm aware."

Chapter 11
Yep, That's Mutual

Monday at six pm, Valerie went to pick up Caleb at his house for their next date. She drummed her fingers on the steering wheel as she rehearsed what she was going to say as soon as they were alone together.

Caleb, I want you to kiss me.

That wasn't bad, but it lacked the necessary oomph.

Caleb, you complete idiotic moron, I want you to kiss me, you dolt.

That was better, but it seemed to lack the romantic mood.

Caleb, would you like to kiss me?

Followed up with coyly upturned eyes, and leaning forward breathlessly . . .

Yeah, that ought to work. Surely he couldn't be *that* dense.

Satisfied with her plan, Valerie got out of the car, walked to the front door, and rung the doorbell.

A middle-aged white man answered the door. "Oh, you must be Caleb's date. I'll go get him. I think he's still doing his hair."

Valerie's mouth gaped open. *It's him! I know that guy!!*

Yep, That's Mutual

It was one of the two people with the unnamed connection to her that she'd found at the office building. She could even smell the unnamed connection right now, because she hadn't talked for several minutes. She'd been chatting to a guy at the gas station while filling up her van a few minutes ago, which was why her range wasn't larger.

What was he doing *here?*

"Caleb!" the man called up the stairs. "Your date is here!"

"What's she doing fifteen minutes early?!" a panicked voice yelled from upstairs. "She's usually late!"

Valerie smirked. *Maybe I should be early more often. I like him being panicked about looking good for me.*

She inhaled deeply, but her range wasn't quite far enough to stretch upstairs to see whether the mutual-crush connection had grown any more yet, more's the pity. Maybe she should've kept her mouth shut on the way here, but she hadn't expected to need to smell things. Oh, well.

"'Scuse me!" Valerie said to the white man. "Who're you? I don't think I've met you before."

"Oh, I'm Steven," he said. "I'm Caleb's father."

Valerie tried not to look disbelieving.

Steven seemed to be trying to suppress a smile. "Yes, I know we don't look very alike. He looks more like his mother."

Boy, she wished she had more range, so she could tell whether they were blood related! Still, she knew Caleb had a mom and one sister, and she'd been able to tell he had three obvious blood relative connections in town at the start, so it seemed a safe bet.

Only parents and siblings had a blood relative scent that was strong enough to be obvious. Once you got a generation removed, like grandparents or uncles or aunts, it was significantly dimmer, and you had to go looking for it. Two generations apart, such as cousins, and it was generally too faint to be discernable at all.

Come to think of it, she also hadn't smelled any adopted family connections between Caleb and anyone else at the start, so yeah, the two had to be blood relatives. They just didn't look like it in the least.

Good, she'd solved that, even though her range was currently pitiful.

Now to figure out why Caleb's dad was one of the people with the unnamed connection.

And hang on! Did that mean Caleb would know what the unnamed connection was?

Valerie grinned, rearranging her plans rapidly.

She made casual conversation with his father in the kitchen while waiting for Caleb, making sure to avoid any mention of her nomadic lifestyle in case Caleb hadn't mentioned that and his dad would object.

She tried to crack a few jokes to pass the time, but the man didn't react to them at all. It was like trying to talk to a plank of wood. No wonder he drove Caleb crazy.

It took Caleb another ten minutes to run down the stairs, looking frantic and ticked off — until he noticed Valerie watching him from the kitchen, at which time he immediately slowed down and sauntered at an unhurried pace to the coat closet to grab his jacket.

Oh, yeah, you're playing it soooooo cool, Valerie snickered.

"Well, ready to go?" she asked him, holding out her hand.

He grabbed it. "Yep, let's go. Bye, Dad!"

"Have a good time," his father said seriously.

The door shut behind them, and they headed to the van.

"Hey, did you know that your dad seems to have no sense of humor?" Valerie commented as they got in.

Caleb looked a bit shifty-eyed. "Uh, yeah. I've noticed that."

They put on their seat belts. Valerie backed out of the driveway. She waited until they were several minutes away from the house and he couldn't escape easily before she said, casually, "So your dad and I seem to have something in common, and I want you to tell me what it is."

"Huh?!" Caleb stared at her in bafflement. "Is this a riddle or something?"

"You tell me. I don't know what it is, but I know that it's something, and I'm thinking you probably do."

Caleb gave her a blank look.

Valerie hesitated. She'd tried to explain this to people before, but no one had ever gotten it. And she'd established that Caleb was dense. Still, he might manage to understand it if he already knew more than she did.

"Okay," she said, pulling over to the side of the road and turning off the van. "There's a dictionary in the glove compartment. Get it out."

"Okay," Caleb said, looking mystified. He leaned forward and found it. "What do I do now?"

"There are four words with sticky notes right under them. Find them."

Caleb flipped through. "Connection, magic, power, smell." He looked up. "Is this a treasure hunt or something?"

"Sort of." Valerie held up a finger. "Okay. The sticky notes have numbers on them. I want you to finish my sentence for me by reading the word with that number. 'I can' — one."

"Smell."

"Two."

"Connection."

"Pluralize it."

"Connections."

"'I think it's a' — three."

"Magic."

"Four."

"No way, you're one of the cursed!" Caleb exclaimed.

"YES!" Valerie pumped her fists in triumph. "Finally I'm getting somewhere! Tell me what's going on, please!"

"Whoa," Caleb said in amazement. "You must be one of the lost cursed. Which one are you?"

"Given that I have no clue what you're talking about, why don't you tell me?"

"Okay." Caleb slammed the dictionary shut. "Tell me your birthday."

"Why, you want to buy me a present or something?"

"I'm trying to figure out your zodiac sign."

"Oh, I know what that is. It's Cancer. Stupidest zodiac *ever.*"

"Really?" Caleb asked with a huge grin. "Why's that?"

"Oh, please. Where do I even start?" Valerie wrinkled her nose. "First of all, it sounds like a disease that nobody wants. Second, the sign is a *crab*, of all things. Third, do you know what it says my personality's supposed to be?"

"What?" Caleb asked with a grin.

Valerie put on a mocking tone. "'Emotional and sensitive. Cares deeply about family and home. A shy introvert who's highly intuitive.' Gaaaaaaag."

Caleb burst out laughing. "Yeah, that's not you!"

"Ya don't say! I once found this book with advice for people with my birthday, which is June twenty-fourth, by the way, so feel free to buy me presents, and yes that's a hint, so do it, and it said I'm way too nice and ought to develop a little healthy selfishness." She snorted. "I was like, 'Oh, great! That sounds fun! So when do I start?' The friend I was with nearly fell over laughing."

Caleb slapped his knee. "That's fantastic! You have no idea how great that is!"

"Why?" Valerie asked, screwing up her face. "It's irritating."

"Before I tell you, is there anything else you want to rant about with your zodiac sign? I'm asking 'cause I find this conversation hilarious."

"Nope, that's it. As far as I'm concerned, the whole concept is bunk. Why'd you bring it up, anyway?"

Caleb sobered. "Because, as far as you and my dad are concerned, and a few other people in town . . . it's not bunk."

"Huh?" Valerie gave him a skeptical look. "I just told you I'm nothing like Cancer."

"Yeah, but you're gonna be turned into one." Caleb looked very serious now. "What you've got is a curse. You have the Cancer curse." He paused. "Actually, do me a favor and repeat those words. Say, 'I have the Cancer curse.'"

Valerie was baffled. "Okaaaay. I have the —"

The last two words wouldn't come out. It was exactly what happened when she tried to say "smell" or "connections."

"What was that?!" she screamed.

"Yup." Caleb didn't look amused anymore. He looked grim. "You have it, all right. I'm sorry, Valerie. You've got the same thing my dad has, and the same thing I'm gonna get when he dies."

"Which is what?" Valerie asked, alarmed.

"A zodiac curse. They all work the same way. The curse will try to change your personality into the ideal whatever-yours-is — in this case, that's Cancer — and once it succeeds, you'll die."

She processed that news for a few seconds.

"Well, forget *that!*" Valerie exclaimed. "How do I get rid of it?"

"Unfortunately, there's no way to do that."

"You're kidding!"

"Wish I were. I told you my dad hates travel? Yeah, that's because the Sagittarius curse is trying to make him love it. Your curse is probably going to make you really clingy and sentimental and wanting to settle down sooner or later."

"Ewwww." Valerie shuddered. "I don't want that."

"Good. The only way to fight it *is* to not want that."

"So it's possible to fight it?" Valerie asked sharply.

"Oh, yeah. If you fight the personality changes of your curse long and hard, you might live twenty years. It'll succeed in the end and kill you, but if you're really lucky, you can make it twenty years after getting a curse. Usually the norm's closer to five or ten."

Valerie slouched down in her chair. "Well, this royally stinks, and it's not what I was hoping it would turn out to be."

"Yep," Caleb said. "I hear ya."

They were silent for a few seconds, which was all Valerie could stand.

"Why can't I say stuff?" she demanded.

"Oh, the curse won't let you talk about it. Not directly."

"How about this?" Valerie poked her nose. "Why can't I talk about this?"

"Oh, right, your power," Caleb said. "Every cursed person has one. Yours was to smell . . . uh . . . what was it again?"

"I can't say the word, Caleb!"

He checked the words with the sticky notes. "Connections."

"That's it."

"What does that even mean?"

"It means mutual stuff," Valerie said. "Between people."

"Like, for example?"

"Hard to give an example," Valerie grumbled. She couldn't say any of the names she came up with for things she smelled. "Okay, let's take your mom and dad. What do you think they feel about each other?"

Caleb thought about it. "Love."

"Yup, that's something I can tell is there."

"Respect."

"Less obvious, but yeah."

"I guess friendship?"

"Yep, that's one of the obvious ones."

"Am I missing any?" Caleb asked.

"Probably loads, but you get the idea. I can't sense anything about individuals, only what's between them."

"Huh." Caleb paused. "What's between us?"

Valerie grinned. "Good question."

"Can't say it, huh?"

"Nope, but you can guess, and I can tell you if you're right." Valerie paused. "My range is only a few inches right now, though, so I'll have to get really close so I can tell. Is that okay?"

"Yeah, that's fine," Caleb said.

She took off her seat belt, stepped over to his side, snuggled onto his lap, and put her head on his shoulder.

Yep. She could definitely smell the connections now.

"Go ahead," she said. "Guess."

"Okay." Caleb thought about it. "I think you're hot."

"Yep, that's one of them."

"Cool." Caleb grinned. "So that goes both ways."

"Obviously, since I've told you that before." She punched him in the shoulder. "C'mon, give me something harder."

"Okay. Lessee." Caleb thought for a minute. "I think you're fun to be around."

"Yup, that's one of 'em."

Yep, That's Mutual

"I also think that —" Caleb broke off. "Hang on a second. This is really unfair. If I make a guess and you say it's not there, that means it's one-sided and now you know about it!"

"C'mon, Caleb," Valerie said, running her hand across his chin. "How much do you *really* think is one-sided here?"

He looked at her for a minute. A grin drifted across his face. "Okay. I like you."

"Yep, that's mutual."

"More than just as a friend."

"Yep, that's mutual."

"More than anyone I've ever dated."

"Yep, that's mutual."

"More than anyone else I've ever met."

"Yep, that's mutual."

"You're the only one I want to be with."

"Yep, that's mutual."

"Maybe for the rest of my life."

"Yep, that's mutual."

"I think I might even . . . love you."

"Yep, that's mutual," she whispered.

The mutual-crush connection had turned into a mutual-in-love connection while they were talking.

"Wow." He looked a little stunned. "That's really cool."

Valerie smiled and traced his jaw with her finger. "Yep, it is."

"Well!" Caleb said, sitting up straight and clapping his hands. "Let's go back and tell my dad about you! He'll be so excited that we've found one of the lost cursed!"

Urrrrrrrrrrrrrrgh! Valerie wanted to punch him.

How many obvious openings was Caleb going to miss to kiss her?

Chapter 12
The One Who's Perfect

On Wednesday right after school, they were supposed to have another board game night with Alex's mom, but when they arrived at the apartment riding Sir Horse, she was gone.

"Mom?" Alex called, walking down the hallway as Amanda sat on the couch. "Mom?"

"Maybe she's running an errand?" Amanda asked.

"I'll call her and ask." Alex pulled his phone out of his pocket. He swiped through it as he sat next to her on the couch. "Oh — she sent me a text fifteen minutes ago. I didn't see it."

Amanda read it over his shoulder.

Sorry, my boss is making me stay an extra hour because a coworker didn't show up for their shift. I'll be there in about an hour and fifteen minutes. Behave.

Alex sent a reply. *Okay.*

Another text showed up a few seconds later. *You might want to send Xander to drop off my library books.*

"Oh, is Xander home already?" Amanda asked with surprise. "I assumed he was still at school."

"He doesn't always go," Alex said. "I'll check. Wait here for a minute."

He walked down the hallway and into the bedroom. He came out a second later, holding the door open. "Yeah, he's here."

Xander sauntered out. "Hello, Amanda! Great to see you!"

"Hello, Xander," she said in a chilly tone.

". . . Oh," Xander said, turning pink and looking down at his feet. "Do you prefer me this way? I mean, if you like me better this way . . ."

"NO!" Amanda shouted. "Stop pretending to be Alex!"

Xander strode over to the couch. He flopped down next to her. "C'mon, admit it. I'm just as good as the real thing."

"You are not!"

"I might even improve upon it."

"There's nothing to improve on!" Amanda snapped. "He's perfect just how he is!"

"Ooh, 'perfect'?" Xander grinned. "You're perfect now, Alex."

Alex's face was red. "No, I'm not."

"Amanda said it, so it has to be true." Xander was grinning, but his eyes looked oddly serious.

"Would you please go take Mom's books to the library?" Alex asked tightly.

"Oh, no. No, no," Xander said with a huge grin. "I wouldn't dream of leaving you alone here together. I'll be a chaperone."

Alex looked disbelieving.

"Don't worry, I'll be the best chaperone ever!" Xander put his arm around Amanda's shoulders and stage-whispered, "That means I'll completely ignore everything you do."

Amanda leapt up from the couch and glared at him.

Xander responded by lying down and propping his feet up against an armrest. "Great. Comfy couch all to myself. Now where are you two going to sit?"

"On you," Alex threatened.

"Oh, yeah? I kick."

This resulted in a brief but triumphant battle in which Alex regained control of the couch and shoved Xander off it.

"Now go return Mom's library books," Alex ordered.

"Fiiiiiiine," Xander said, and got up off the floor. He headed down the hallway, opened the door to a bedroom all the way at the end, and collected a stack of plastic-covered hardcover books from the top of a dresser. "I sure hope these are it, because if not, the library's about to get a donation."

As Xander left the apartment, Amanda sat down next to Alex and took his hand.

"Do you and your mom read a lot of books?" she asked.

"Yeah, I'm fond of medieval history and epic fantasy."

"What does your mom read?"

"Mostly romance novels."

"And Xander?"

"He reads the same books I do."

Amanda grinned. "When he was pretending to be you, and he said he thought of himself as a knight while he's riding Sir Horse, was he talking for you or himself?"

"Both," Alex admitted with an embarrassed grin. "We're not *that* different, y'know."

"To me, you seem like night and day."

"We are, but . . . we didn't used to be. When I was a kid, even my mom couldn't tell us apart."

"What happened?" Amanda asked curiously.

Alex looked sad. "Time passed. I miss the days when Xander and I always thought the same way."

"I've never had a twin," Amanda said, "but I can imagine."

They sat in silence for a few minutes.

"Hey, can I read your poetry?" Amanda asked.

"No!" Alex's shoulders hunched. "It's terrible!"

"There's nothing wrong with being terrible. It's just the first step to getting better."

Alex hesitated. "Well . . . maybe I'll show you *one*."

He got up and walked down the hallway to the bedroom that he seemed to share with Xander. He came back a minute later with a hardcover journal that had an illustration of a knight rescuing a lady on the cover.

The One Who's Perfect

He sat down next to her, opened the book to a page with four lines, and handed it over. "This one," he said, his face red. "Don't read the others."

It said:

> Her eyes are like lanterns,
> brightening the dark of my night.
> Her lips are a beacon,
> drawing me into the light.

"That's beautiful," Amanda breathed. "I love it."

"You do?" His eyes were wide and scared.

She nodded.

"It's . . . it's about you."

"What?" Amanda gasped and looked back at it. "Really? Oh, wow! B-but — my lips are hardly beacons. They're leathery and peeling because I chew them too much, and —"

Alex leaned forward and kissed her.

It lasted only a second before he pulled back, looking nervous.

"Was that okay?" he asked, his face redder than ever.

She scooted closer and kissed him again.

He rubbed his hands up and down her arms.

She kissed his cheek, then his neck, then his ear, then his neck.

His hands reached for the front of her shirt.

"Not there!" Amanda said, pushing them away.

He rubbed the small of her back instead.

She shivered as she ran her fingers through his hair and kissed his forehead, his nose, then his mouth.

He offered the tip of his tongue, and she met it with hers. It sent a frission of thrills down her back.

His hands were now on her chest.

"Alex!" Amanda yelped, jumping back. "Not *there!*"

He pulled them away. "You don't like that?"

"Right! Don't do that!"

"Sorry." He hesitated. "Can I kiss you again?"

"Please do."

He grinned, and they got back to it.

She was stroking the sides of his face as they kissed when she suddenly became aware that there was a hand sliding up her thigh under her skirt.

"*ALEX!*" Amanda screamed, leaping up from the couch. "*NO!*"

"But I just —"

"'Just'?! 'Just'?!"

The front door jingled for a second as it was unlocked, then opened. "Well, I hope you like Chaucer, because I checked out *The Canterbury Tales!*" Xander proclaimed, waving a book around with a puckish grin. "I'm thinking I'll read you 'The Cook's Tale' —"

Amanda marched over to the front door and snatched her coat from the floor. "I'm going home."

"Wait, you screwed up?" Xander said to his twin incredulously.

"Shut up," Alex hissed through clenched teeth.

"*You* screwed up?"

"Shut up!"

"You're the one who's supposed to be perfect!"

"Well, I'm not perfect, am I?!" Alex shouted. He stormed down the hallway and slammed the door to their bedroom.

There was an awkward silence for a minute.

"Get out of the way," Amanda said coldly. "I'm going."

Xander moved out of the doorway. "Let me drive you home."

"I don't want anything from you," she snapped.

"It's a really long walk, and it's cold out. Let me drive you home."

"Fine," Amanda said, shoving her hands into her pockets. The wind coming through the doorway *was* cold. "But don't you dare flirt with me."

"Wouldn't dream of it," Xander said seriously.

Riding on Sir Horse with Xander was very different from riding with Alex. It was tense, and stiff, and awkward, and tears kept leaking from Amanda's eyes, which made her face cold.

They arrived outside her apartment building. Amanda got off the motorcycle in stony silence.

The One Who's Perfect

"Hey," Xander said, turning to look at her. "Don't be too hard on Alex, okay? I dunno what he did, but I know he loves you. He really, really, really, really loves you."

"He needs to learn some self-control," Amanda hissed.

Xander flinched as if she'd slapped him.

She stormed up the stairs to reach the door of her family's apartment, got out her key, and let herself in. As she did, she heard the sound of laughter in the kitchen.

She walked past the kitchen to get to her bedroom, seeing her parents cooking dinner together and making silly puns about silverware. It looked like they were preparing lasagna.

Amanda struggled to hold back her tears. She didn't want to talk about what had just happened.

She got to her bedroom and tossed her coat on the floor. Then she headed to the bathroom, where she closed the door, stood in front of the mirror, and turned on her power.

Alex's painting had moved to the center, with the wall of twelve blank canvases behind it. But now it was no longer on the easel. It had slipped and fallen to the floor.

The contents of his cityscape had changed, too. There was a giant crack down the middle, and soot was flying out of it. The whirlwind of soot made him look like Xander. All of the buildings were spattered with black, and the deep forest green one was so caked with it that she could no longer see the pillars.

The soot was lust.

Amanda turned off her power, flung the bathroom door open, ran to her bedroom, shut and locked the door, and flopped onto her bed. She buried her face in her pillow to muffle the sound, and then cried hysterically.

∼∼

Xander got home and opened the bedroom door. He found Alex crying and wiping his face and writing in his journal.

"Alex," Xander began.

"Go away!"

"We're way over the time limit —"

"Stay away from me!" Alex said fiercely. "I don't want you with these memories until I've sorted through them!"

Xander hesitated. "Okay. You're the boss."

He shut the door and went to the living room, where he sat on the couch, tapping his foot on the ground.

Alex had screwed up. *Alex* had screwed up. That shouldn't be possible. Alex was always right. Whenever they disagreed, it was because Xander was wrong. That was the law of reality.

Alex was the man he wanted to be, the man he was trying to be, and the man he could never be.

If *Alex* had screwed up . . . the world was broken.

If *Alex* got it wrong, there was no hope for Xander.

Chapter 13

The Significance of What He Just Said

In the morning, when her alarm clock rang, Amanda turned it off and dragged herself out of bed, exhausted from crying all night.

She got up earlier than her parents did because she went to seminary before school. So at least she didn't have to see them before she left. She wouldn't have to try to pretend she was fine. Or else admit that she'd ignored all their advice about avoiding potentially treacherous situations and then gotten burned in exactly the way they'd warned her she might.

She'd avoided them last night, too. She knew they'd notice something was wrong, and she didn't want to talk about it.

Not yet. It was too raw, too painful.

She'd been betrayed.

She'd been violated.

How could she ever trust him again?

She didn't want to break up with him. He was so perfect in every other way. But at the same time . . . how could she *not*?

How could a relationship work if he assumed doing that was okay?

Why had he ruined what had been so perfect?

She didn't go to the mirror to check her reflection. She didn't want to see what Alex looked like now. The thought of doing so made her stomach knot.

Either it would be the same as it was originally, which would mean she'd been fooled and this could happen again, or it would be how it was yesterday, which would mean *he* was ruined. She couldn't bear to think about either possibility.

As she pulled on a shirt, Amanda's eyes fell on a poster her mom had made her last week. It was a cartoon of a giant-sized Amanda stepping on a bunch of scared-looking bugs that were each labeled with a negative trait of Aquarius.

Runs from problems, said one.

Denies making mistakes, said another.

Doesn't understand others' feelings, said a third.

Pride, said a fourth.

Selfishness, said a fifth.

And the sixth said, *Slow to forgive.*

Amanda stared at the poster for a long, long time.

"But that's not fair," she objected. "It's *not* my fault! I mean, okay, maybe I got a little too into the kissing . . ."

Denies making mistakes, the second bug jeered.

"And besides, I can't trust him again!"

The sixth little bug seemed to taunt her. *Slow to forgive.*

Amanda turned her back on the poster and finished getting dressed.

〜〜〜
〜〜〜

So of *course* the morning's seminary lesson was on Mosiah 26. Of course it was. And of course the teacher decided to focus most of the lesson on the verses about forgiveness.

Amanda left the teacher's house trailing after the other five students, three of whom were walking to school from here. The teacher's house was only a ten-minute walk from the Greenfell, which was helpful to the four of them who went there. The other two had their moms drive them to their schools.

The Significance of What He Just Said

The three students ahead of her chatted with each other as they walked. Amanda didn't say anything.

It wasn't that she didn't like the other students in seminary. They seemed nice, and she saw them in church every week. She just didn't know them. She hadn't really made the effort to get to know anyone in town except for Alex.

Maybe they'd moved too fast.

Maybe she should have made other friends, as well.

Maybe she shouldn't have dated a nonmember.

Maybe she shouldn't have trusted what her power told her about Alex in the first place.

She just didn't know.

"Amanda," said a quiet voice behind her.

She turned, and Alex was walking behind her.

Amanda stopped and looked at him. The other students receded down the sidewalk, leaving the two of them alone.

"Your parents said you'd be here," he said. "I went to your place to find you."

"Why?" Amanda asked quietly.

"I want to apologize. I should've stopped when you said to."

"Yeah," she said. "You should've."

"I should've." He nodded. "It was my fault. I'm sorry."

Amanda closed her eyes and drew in a deep breath. Did forgiveness mean you had to give someone a second chance? She wasn't sure, but she knew she wanted to.

"Alex," she said carefully, opening her eyes, "where do you think our relationship is going? Be honest."

His face reddened. "Do I have to say it?"

"Please."

He looked down at his feet. "I — I guess I assumed we'd sleep together at some point. Not necessarily yesterday, but . . . sometime."

Amanda inhaled. "Okay. We need to talk about that. I'm not doing that until I'm married. Or anything else like it."

"Ohhh." Realization dawned on Alex's face. "So that's why."

"Yeah, that's why."

"I should've asked."

"I should've told you."

"If you want me to keep my hands off you, I will," Alex said.

"Thank you," Amanda said quietly.

They were silent for a moment.

"Amanda," Alex said, "where do *you* think the relationship is going?"

She swallowed. It was hard to admit it. "I guess I thought we might get married someday."

"Okay. We need to talk about *that.*" Alex looked very sad. "I don't think I'm going to live that long."

Amanda stared at him in shock. "What? Why not?"

"I've got a — condition," he said carefully. "It's the same one my dad had. No one with it has ever lived longer than twenty years, and I got it when I was a baby, and I'm eighteen and a half now, so . . . ."

Amanda stopped breathing. "What's your birthday?"

"June eighth —" His eyes went wide. "You know."

"I do know."

"How do you know?"

"Because I've got one, too."

"*NO!*" he screamed. "No! No, no, no! Not *you!*"

"I got it —"

"You're supposed to be *yourself!*" he howled. "Not changed! Not changed! *Not changed!*"

"I *am* myself!" Amanda cried. "I got it three months ago!"

"Oh." Alex inhaled in gasps. "Oh. Oh. Oh. Oh. Ohhhhh. You're the new one. Steven's relative. The one he wants us to meet in a few days."

Amanda nodded.

"I should've realized," Alex moaned. "He said the new one was named Amanda. I just assumed it was someone his age."

"I could've realized it, too," Amanda said slowly. "Your mom said your dad changed rapidly."

Alex winced. "Yeah. The personality changes are the worst part of the whole thing."

The Significance of What He Just Said

"Not the worst part." Amanda's stomach knotted. "I probably won't even see much difference. I'm pretty much where it wants me to be already."

Alex inhaled sharply. "Oh no."

She nodded.

"Nooooo," he groaned. "The last time that happened, the man died in only six months."

"That's pretty much what Steven told me."

"But at least you don't have to worry about being changed!" Alex exclaimed, taking both of her hands and gripping them. "It'll be shorter, but it might be better that way!"

Amanda felt the hairs on the back of her neck raise. "Better than what?"

"Than spending eighteen years fighting its mind-control, feeling yourself slip a little more each day. Sometimes I wonder if it's even worth staying alive to keep on living like this!"

Amanda could scarcely breathe. "Wait a minute. Are you *not* yourself?"

"Not . . . usually," Alex said quietly.

"Then what *is* your natural personality?"

Alex hesitated for a long time. At last, he drew both sets of hands up to his chest. "This."

"But you just said —"

"Amanda," Alex said, very carefully, "I'm cursed."

"I know."

"I think you missed the significance of what I just said. *I'm cursed.*"

Her eyes widened. "You're *not?*"

Cursed people couldn't say they were cursed! Had he been lying to her?!

"Oh no." Alex shook his head. "I am. Just not right now."

"What does that mean?" she asked slowly.

"It means right now, I'm Alex. When I'm cursed, I go by the name Xander. Xander isn't my twin. He's my doppelganger."

Chapter 14
Beside Himself

Xander had been Alex's doppelganger since he was a baby.

His mother knew about it, of course. So did his uncle and aunt, because their ten-year-old son was Alex's heir, and they needed to know that Xander would die at the same time as Alex. They were the only ones his mother had told.

All of the zodiac cursed and some of the heirs when he was a child had known, because he'd used his power in front of them and they had talked about it openly back then, but he'd sworn them all to secrecy when he was ten, before the newest cursed person had met them.

Aaron had been the last of the cursed to know what Alex's power was, and he'd died six months ago. That meant only Alex's mother, aunt, and uncle knew now.

And Amanda.

Now she knew.

Amanda didn't seem to understand. "What are you talking about? He's your twin."

"No, he isn't."

"He's a separate person!"

"No, he isn't."

"But I've seen the two of you together!"

"That's my power. I can split myself into two bodies. When I merge back, I have the memories of both."

"O-oh," she gasped, sinking down to the sidewalk, still holding his hands. "O-oh. You're Xander."

"I'm afraid so."

"How often are you Alex?" she asked, looking up at him.

"Not as often as you might think." Alex knelt down beside her, gripping both her hands for dear life. He felt like, if he released her, he'd drown. "I'm Xander for twenty-three hours out of every day. I spend most of that time pretending to be Alex."

She looked stunned. "Why not be Alex all the time?"

"Because using my power advances the curse. So does *not* using it, because I start to forget how I think. So I only spend an hour out of every day split. It's a self-imposed time limit. It's the best way I know to fight the curse. The only time I'm really me is when I'm split and Alex. Alex doesn't have the curse. When I'm merged, I'm cursed, which means I'm Xander."

"Pretending to be Alex," she whispered.

"Pretending to be Alex."

"At the grocery store . . ." she whispered.

"Merged."

"At the cafeteria . . ."

"Merged."

"How often have you been Xander when we were together?!" She looked distressed.

"Most of it," Alex said. "You only noticed the two times."

"Alex, I . . ." She let go of his hands. "I don't know what to think! I don't *like* Xander!"

"Good!" Alex said emphatically, seizing them back again. "I wouldn't want to be with you if you did! *Please* hate him, and please love *me!*"

Amanda stared at him for a long moment.

"I do," she said at last.

"You do?" he whispered.

She nodded. "I love you."

"I love you, too." He breathed raggedly.

"Do you want to kiss me?" Amanda whispered.

He kissed her, and she kissed him back, and it was beautiful and perfect.

There were whistles and catcalls from across the street.

They broke off and looked over. A group of teenage boys had just walked past.

Amanda's face was pink. "We — we — I think we're going to be late for school."

"I guess we'd better walk quickly," Alex said.

"I don't want to walk quickly."

"Then let's be late."

She kissed the side of his face, and he kissed her lips.

They let go of each other's hands to get up, then laced fingers together again to walk at a strolling snail's pace. They walked in the opposite direction of the school.

"When were the times you were Alex?" Amanda asked softly.

"The day we met. Our first date. The second half of the date when you met my mom. And, well . . . last night."

It was still a painful memory, even with her walking beside him now. He hadn't expected her to reject him. He'd thought she would enjoy it as much as he did.

Amanda looked shocked. "Were those the only times?"

He nodded.

"How could I have been so fooled?" she moaned.

Alex shook his head. "It's not a question of being fooled, Amanda. The only time I let Xander behave the way I want to is when I'm split. When I'm merged, I'm trying to be Alex. When I'm with you, I've gotten closer to it than I have for years."

"I — I have an awkward question." She bit her lip.

"Yeah?"

"Does Xander love me?"

"Yes," Alex said softly. "Exactly the same way I do."

"The same feelings?"

"Mm-hm. We're the same man."

Amanda was silent as they walked for a few minutes.

"That has to hurt," she said at last. "The fact that I don't love him."

"It does," Alex said. "But in a very good way. It gives me a reason to fight to stay Alex."

She stared at him. "You mean I'm helping you survive?"

"There's no doubt. I was clinging to the edge of a precipice through sheer determination. I didn't know how much longer I could last before falling in. But if you love me as Alex, it makes me want to pull myself *out*."

"Is that possible?" Amanda whispered.

"I don't care if it's possible or not." Alex spoke with quiet iron in his voice. "If you want me to live, I'll keep on living for you."

". . . Wow," Amanda whispered.

They walked on in silence, swinging their hands together.

"I guess I should have figured it out," Amanda said at last. "'Alex' and 'Xander' are both nicknames for 'Alexander.'"

Alex grinned wryly. "Yeah. I didn't do a good job of naming myself, did I? In my defense, I was a little kid at the time."

"Do people comment on that a lot?"

"So often," Alex sighed. "I usually tell people his full name is Alessandro. I had my middle name legally changed to that so I'm not lying when I say it."

"What was it before?"

"Shadrach. My father's name."

And given that his father had succumbed to the curse in only a year and a half because he'd enjoyed his luck power so much, Alex hadn't minded extinguishing him as a namesake. He hadn't told his mother that was the biggest reason he was changing it, though. He didn't want to hurt her.

They went back to silence as they walked for awhile, their hands swinging together.

"How does the memory sharing work?" Amanda asked. "Do Alex's memories go to Alex and Xander's go to Xander when you split?"

"No." Alex shook his head. "Once I merge, I have all my memories, and when I split, both versions of me do, too."

"Can you split more than once?"

"No, I only have two bodies."

"'Only,'" she said with amusement.

"'Only.'" He smiled back.

"What made you decide to go by 'Alex'?"

Alex took a deep breath. "That's a . . . very long story. Do you want to hear it?"

"I want to hear anything you're willing to tell me."

He hesitated for a moment. It wasn't exactly a happy story, and he wasn't sure how he felt about sharing it.

But this was Amanda. She could know.

"When I was little," Alex said slowly, "my doppelganger and I were interchangeable. I was my own favorite playmate, and I never wanted to play with other children. That's the reason why I had to repeat kindergarten, actually. My social skills were severely lacking."

"I'm sure you were adorable," she said gently. "You certainly were in those pictures." She paused and looked thunderstruck. "Wait, those were *all* of you, weren't they?"

"Yeah." Alex chuckled.

"Even the one with the two babies!"

"Both me, yes."

"And the two little boys with the blocks!"

"To tell you the truth, I'm pretty sure the uncursed me was the one with the hammer," Alex said with an embarrassed laugh. "Like I said, we were interchangeable back then."

"Wow." Amanda shook her head. "That's mind-blowing."

"I know. It's still weird to me sometimes, and I've been splitting and merging for as long as I can remember. Although, as a kid, it was weird to me that other people *couldn't* do that. My earliest memory was standing in a crib with a drooping diaper, watching my mother change the other me's drooping diaper and wondering why she didn't just split and change us both."

Amanda burst into giggles.

"Yeah." Alex cracked a smile. "If it'd stayed that way, things would've been great."

Amanda sobered. "What happened?"

"Well," Alex said, "on my fifth birthday, I was given a Lego set that I really wanted to build."

She gave him a puzzled look.

"Meanwhile, my doppelganger wanted to play tag. I kept trying to build it, and he kept knocking it over and trying to drag me into the living room. He wouldn't even merge when I told him to. That had never happened before. I was terrified." Alex swallowed. "It was the first time I ever remember him disagreeing with me. Before that, we'd always seemed to have two copies of the same mind. I didn't even learn to talk until I was four because it seemed unnecessary. If I wanted something, so did the other me, and we could usually work together to get it."

Amanda was silent.

"I went to Mom, crying. She sat me down on her lap and told me about the curse. She said as I got older, my doppelganger would become more and more different, and the ways in which he changed would be dangerous to me." Alex's voice shook. "I cried about it for days."

Amanda nodded, looking teary-eyed.

"Soon after that, I started using 'Alexander' to describe the merged me and 'Alex' and 'Xander' for the split mes."

"But . . ." Amanda began.

"I know," Alex said quietly. "I'm not done. Back then, I thought the merged me was the real me, and the other two were halves. I used the nicknames interchangeably because I thought it didn't matter which one was which, even though I knew one was cursed and one wasn't. Then one day, when I was ten, I realized that the merged me thought the same way as the split me with the curse. That was when I realized that the real me wasn't the merged one at all. It was the one who was different from both."

Amanda nodded.

"That was shattering. It meant that Alexander didn't exist. Only Alex and Xander."

"Right," Amanda said slowly.

"So I flipped a coin to decide whether the real me would go by the name 'Alex' or 'Xander.' It landed on heads. And I've been Alex ever since."

They walked on in silence.

"You're amazing," Amanda said.

He looked over at her. "What?"

"Alex, you just told me that you spent five years under a kind of mind-control that many people succumb to and die of within five years, and you were still barely affected."

"I wouldn't say 'barely,'" Alex said, his face heating up. "It was a noticeable change by that point."

"And you didn't even start fighting it until you were ten."

"No, no, I was fighting it when I was five," Alex said quickly, shaking his head. "My mom's the one who's amazing. She was training me in self-control and patience and all kinds of things from before I can even remember. She knew I would need them to survive, and the curse would be trying to steal them from me. You have no idea how much time she spent and how much work she had to go to. I literally owe her my life, and more."

"So you had a wonderful teacher," Amanda said.

"Yes."

"And she had a wonderful student."

"I don't think I get any credit for it." Alex shook his head.

"I think you do." She stopped, let go of his hand, wrapped her arms around him, and kissed him.

He kissed her back hungrily, then more carefully, then moved his hands to the sides of her face, where they'd be safer than where they wanted to go.

He wished so much that she wanted to sleep with him.

Oh, well. There was no point in regretting what wouldn't change.

"I love you so much," Alex whispered.

"I love you, too," Amanda said. "Thank you for telling me all that. I bet it wasn't easy."

"It wasn't." He smiled slightly. "You're welcome."

Amanda bit her lip. "You know . . . we *could* get married."

Alex froze. "What?"

"We could." She swallowed. "If you want to. Soon."

"Wow, I want to," he breathed. "Are you sure?"

She nodded.

"How soon?" he asked. His heart was racing.

"A month?"

"Before school's even over?"

"I don't care about school. I'm clearly not going to college. How about you?"

He breathed in deeply. "I — I do think we should finish. Graduate. We're so close to being done with it already. But i-if you want to get married first, we can get married first."

He could scarcely believe it. Two hours ago, he'd been afraid she'd never want to see him again.

And now this.

"You can keep your hands off my chest for that long, right?" she added with a slight smile.

Alex cringed. "I'm sorry —"

"I know. I was teasing you." She squeezed his hand. "You have more self-control than anyone I've ever met."

"Clearly I don't," Alex said embarrassedly.

"Yes, you do."

"No, I don't."

"You've hung on to your soul for *eighteen and a half years* when the norm is five to ten. This when you got what you have as a *baby,* before your personality was even fully formed. If anyone is capable of doing the impossible, you are. If you've already done that, you can do *anything.*"

Alex was dumbfounded. "Well . . . thank you."

Not for himself, but perhaps she was right.

For *her* . . . he could do anything.

Chapter 15

Black and White

Ringing the doorbell of Ellen's house with one hand while holding Valerie's hand with the other, Caleb looked over at her with a mischievous grin.

She grinned back.

After Caleb's unreasonable obtuseness following their mutual confession of love, which it seemed he still had not recovered from because the imbecile still hadn't kissed her, they had come up with a much more entertaining plan than immediately driving back home and telling his dad about her.

Namely, they were here to crash the meeting with all of the cursed.

A woman answered the door. She gave off all the usual odors for a marriage shared with someone in the house, and she also had blood-family and family-love connections with a second. Presumably her husband and child.

"Hello?" she asked, giving the two of them a puzzled look.

"Hi, I'm Caleb," Caleb said, holding out his hand. "I'm here for the meeting."

The woman blinked. "Are you one of the heirs?"

"Yep. Sagittarius. Steven's my dad."

Now she looked startled. "Steven's your father?"

"Yup." Caleb looked like he was barely suppressing rolling his eyes. He'd commented to Valerie that nobody ever seemed to believe he was mixed-race.

"You don't look at all like —"

"Yes, I know," Caleb said with a straight face. "I've got my mom's nose."

Valerie snickered.

"And who's this?" the woman asked, looking at Valerie.

"She's my girlfriend," Caleb said. "She's coming in, too. Don't worry, she knows about everything."

"Um, I think it's just supposed to be heirs and cursed —"

Valerie smiled and waved cheerfully as they barged past the woman into the house.

There were a bunch of people in the living room, six of whom shared the zodiac-curse connection with each other and Valerie, and the discussion was already well underway. It seemed that Caleb had been right when he'd called her up to complain that she was fifteen minutes late, and hello?!

"This is Ellen," a man was saying, patting the head of the little girl who lived in this house. They shared blood-family and family-love connections. "She's my daughter. Her power is to automate things."

"It's amazing!" the little girl said with satisfaction. "I can get my bed to make itself, and the dishes to do themselves, and —"

"But you don't do those things, right?" the man said sternly. "Because you don't want the curse to advance."

"Noooooo . . ." the little girl muttered.

"Valerie!" Lucy exclaimed from across the room. "What are you doing here?"

Everyone turned to the doorway to look at her and Caleb.

Valerie smiled and waved.

"This is my girlfriend," Caleb said. "She knows everything. Don't mind us, just keep on with your introductions."

"Caleb," his father said with evident exasperation, "you know we don't bring extra people to these."

"Then why do Ellen's parents get to be here?"

"Because we own this house?" Ellen's father said.

"She's a *kid!*" Lucy exclaimed at the same time.

"Just think of Valerie as my plus-one," Caleb said innocently.

"We don't do plus-ones," a woman sitting on a chair by the fireplace said acidly. Valerie assumed this was Catherine, the Leo who was Caleb's dad's boss.

"Yeah, if I don't get to bring my boyfriend, you don't get to bring your girlfriend, Caleb," Lucy put in. "I'd *totally* bring Pablo if I were allowed to. But we don't have space for extra people. It would get too crowded."

Valerie's eyebrows raised. *So Lucy's boyfriend knows about the curse?*

She'd given Caleb a hard time yesterday about how he'd treated Lucy's friend on that infamous double date, and he'd indignantly excused himself from wrongdoing by telling her about Lucy's power and how it worked.

According to Caleb, Lucy's power made any guys she was attracted to feel the same way about her, and her power was the kind that didn't turn off, like Valerie's.

Which explained the hint of the zodiac-curse connection mixed in with the other connections between Lucy and her boyfriend.

"It's not just about space," Alex said quietly from a corner. He was sitting next to Amanda and holding her hand. "It's also about privacy. Not all of us want to talk in front of strangers about these things."

Right, like you have any privacy from me, Valerie thought with a smirk. *I can smell the mild friendship connection you have with Caleb, the mutual-dislike connection you have with Lucy, and the mutual-in-love connection you've got with Amanda.*

Alex was the first cursed person she'd met in town, the one she'd first sniffed out at Greenfell who had been very polite, very distant, and abundantly unhelpful. According to Caleb, the guy didn't talk a whole lot, but he was all right.

Black and White

Amanda raised her hand that wasn't linked with Alex's and waved at Valerie sheepishly.

"Sorry, Caleb," Steven said firmly. "I'm glad you decided to come to the meeting after all, but Valerie needs to wait for you somewhere else."

"Oh," Caleb said, rubbing his chin. "I guess you guys don't want to meet the Cancer, after all. Huh. I thought for sure you'd be interested. Okay, we'll go!"

Valerie and Caleb turned around and headed back towards the door, glancing at each other and trying very hard not to burst into snickers.

Shouts and exclamations darted across the room.

"Oh, wait," Caleb said innocently, turning back around. "Did I forget to mention that part? Valerie's the Cancer. She's one of the lost cursed. She came into town looking for us."

"Hi," Valerie said with a grin, breaking her silence. She'd had enough time sniffing them all out. "It's about time I met you guys. Do I get to stay now?"

Amanda's mouth opened in shock.

Oh, yeah, Valerie remembered. *She didn't know I could talk, did she?*

<div align="center">~~~</div>

A few hours of charts and analysis later, which Lucy and Ellen departed from early to play videogames with each other instead, Valerie was all up to speed.

Everyone seemed amazed at what her power was, which was pretty satisfying. Well, everyone except the Leo who had made all the charts.

"Why couldn't it have been an always-on external informational or always-on internal action one?" Catherine griped. "My chart doesn't need another always-on internal informational example. I've already got mine there."

"Your conclusions are bunk, by the way," Caleb said casually, flipping through the pages. "You don't have enough data points for any of this to be statistically significant."

Catherine drew herself up to her full height. "I'll have you know that —!"

Thus began an epic squabble between Caleb and his dad's boss, which was probably not the wisest move Valerie's boyfriend had ever made, but she found it too entertaining to intervene. Steven, meanwhile, sunk further and further down in his chair, probably hoping nobody would ask him to take sides.

Glancing over at the corner, Valerie noticed Amanda and Alex whispering together. Amanda kissed Alex on the cheek, and he squeezed her hand tightly.

Fine, rub it in that Caleb's too stupid to kiss me, Valerie wanted to grumble.

The meeting ended soon after that, and she and Caleb walked out to the van together. It was late, but there was no way Valerie was taking him home before he had to get back for his curfew.

"So, what'd you think of the other cursed?" Caleb asked as she unlocked the driver's side door and opened it.

Valerie stopped and pondered. "Well, your dad has no sense of humor."

"Yeah, to protect himself from the Sagittarius curse."

"Catherine's very organized."

"She's definitely that."

"Ellen's, I dunno, a kid."

"Kind of a brat, if you ask me."

"Lucy's cool. I like her. Mind you, if she ever tries to go after you again, I'll kill her."

Caleb burst out laughing.

"And Alex and Amanda . . . I dunno. Not much impression of them. They're sweet together, though."

"We're better," Caleb smirked, raising his eyebrows.

"Really?" Valerie said coyly. "Show me."

"I don't have to," he teased. "I'm sure you can smell it."

"Caleb," Valerie said, seizing him by the shoulders, "moron. Kiss me."

"No."

She stared at him incredulously. "*What?*"

Black and White

"It's not that I don't love you. I really do. It's just that I'm not kissing until I'm married."

She blinked. "Excuse me?!"

"Yeah, and you've made it really hard to keep dodging it, too."

"You've been doing that *on purpose?*"

"Yeah, see, 'cause —"

"For what possible reason?!"

"My grandma and grandpa told me when I was a kid that they had their first kiss at the altar. I thought it seemed really romantic. It also seemed like it would make things way easier. So I decided I'd do that, too."

Valerie flung her arms in the air. "You're unbelievable!"

"It's all black and white this way," Caleb said with satisfaction. "No grey areas. My wife gets everything, and everyone else gets nothing."

Valerie let out an incoherent snarl. She'd said no to plenty of guys before. But she'd never had a guy say no to *her* before. It was infuriating to have the shoe on the other foot.

"What?" he said with a puzzled look. "You know you're the one I'm most likely to ask, right?"

Her fury calmed somewhat. She took a deep breath. "Will you at least hug me? Is that against the rules?"

He hesitated. "Well, not technically, but see, you're really hot, so that seems kind of grey area-ish . . ."

"CALEB, HUG ME!"

Thankfully, he enfolded her in a giant bear hug, allowing her to snuggle in close.

She squeezed him, her head against his chest, breathing in the connections between them. They were delicious and exciting and enticing and doggone it, he wouldn't even let her kiss him!

She just *had* to fall in love with a guy who was a giant pain in the rear.

Chapter 16
Under Construction

"Hey, Alex?" Amanda began as they swung their linked hands between them, fifteen minutes after they left to walk home from the meeting. She paused. "Or should I call you Xander?"

"Call me Alex when there's only one of me, please. That's who I'm trying to be."

She nodded. "Why did Catherine say the thing you do is reading Xander's mind?"

Alex looked uncomfortable. "I didn't lie about it, in case you're wondering. I just refused to say what it was, and some of them jumped to the conclusion that I couldn't say it, so it had to be something that couldn't be described in normal terms."

"So they jumped to telepathy?" That seemed quite a stretch.

"Yeah . . . when I was little, I still had trouble remembering not to use the right pronouns."

"The right pronouns?" Amanda asked curiously.

"Y'know. I'd say 'I' when I was talking about something that had happened to Xander. Or I'd talk about what he thought. They drew their own conclusions from there."

"You must've been *so* adorable as a child."

"Well, my mom thought so," he said, chuckling.

"Of course, technically it wouldn't have been lying to say you could read Xander's mind," Amanda said with amusement.

"Yeah, I can read my own mind just fine," Alex said with a wry grin. "But still, it's kind of the opposite. When there are two of me, that's the only time I *don't* know what I'm thinking. I only find out afterwards from the memories."

"Is that weird?" Amanda asked.

"It's quite often weird."

"Has Xander *ever* gone against you while you were split?" She'd noticed that he didn't seem to be able to say the words *split* or *merged* or *doppelganger* while merged.

"All the time," Alex said. "But only when it's not important. If I tell me to do something, I know I'm serious, and I do it. Alex is always right. I know Alex is always right. Alex has to be right, because otherwise there's no point to anything."

Goosebumps rose on her skin. It was eerie to hear him talk that way, with such matter-of-fact fanatical devotion.

Now that she knew what to look for, she was starting to be able to tell the difference between Alex and Xander even without using her power. The split Alex smiled more often and was more confident. The merged version was always a little more shy and a little more serious, perhaps because he was trying too hard to mimic who the real Alex was.

It wasn't as obvious as a caricature. It was more like a skillful forgery. A forgery that she was trying to treat just like the real thing, even though she knew he wasn't, because he needed her just as much when he was merged as when he was split.

Amanda squeezed her forgery's hand, smiling over at him.

He smiled back.

It wasn't easy to know that the heart behind the hand she was holding was Xander's. But the mind and the will were Alex's. That would have to do.

Still, it was only when Alex was truly himself that she would allow him to kiss her. Or anything else, after they got married.

Amanda's face heated up at the thought.

"Hey," Alex said, stopping. "You never mentioned what you could do at the meeting."

Amanda smiled. "That's right, I didn't."

"In all the fuss about Valerie, nobody asked."

"That's right. And I didn't volunteer it."

He looked at her plaintively. "Won't you tell me what it is?"

Amanda thought about it for a moment. She liked having it as a secret, something she knew that nobody else did. But there was one person she was okay with knowing about it.

"I'll tell Alex," she said.

"Okay?" His eyes brightened eagerly.

"Xander," she said, "I'll tell *Alex*."

He sighed, and his shoulders slumped. "You mean I have to wait for awhile?"

"Unless you can find a place to split near here where no one will notice it."

Abandoning all pretense, Xander's head whipped around with eager excitement. "Hang on!" he said, holding up a finger. "I'll go to the bathroom in that grocery store over there!"

He ran down the sidewalk ahead of her, leaving her behind.

Amanda's shoulders shook with laughter. Xander was such a nut. As a stand-in for her fiancé, he was less than perfect, but at least she didn't feel threatened or offended when he insisted on flirting with her now. She knew he wasn't trying to steal her. He was even more devoted to Alex than he was to her.

And she appreciated it, because it was Xander's devotion that kept Alex alive.

She walked to the grocery store and waited outside the exit. Alex emerged, looking sheepish.

"Sorry I left you behind," he said.

"You're forgiven," she chuckled.

"So . . . will you tell me about your power now?" he asked hopefully.

Amanda grinned. *Well done. Saying the word so I would know for certain it's you.*

Under Construction

Of course, she already had her own way to confirm it, but he didn't know that yet. She turned her power on for a brief moment to make sure, and it was Alex.

"Okay," Amanda said, taking his hands. "You have to promise not to tell anyone else."

"Of course I won't. You have my word."

Of course Xander would know as well as soon as he merged, but in this precious moment, only she and Alex would know.

She let go of one of his hands and tapped under her eye. "I can see you."

Alex looked confused. "I know?"

"I think you missed the significance of what I just said. I can see . . . *you*."

His eyes widened. "You can see . . . *me?*"

She nodded.

"You're not talking about . . . what I look like, are you?"

"Not at all."

"Wow," he whispered. "Can you describe it?"

"I can't." Amanda sighed. *I can't even draw it.* "You know how the limitations work."

"I know," Alex said regretfully. "I figured."

"Maybe I can put it in general terms, though," Amanda said. She thought for a minute, trying to find an appropriate metaphor. "You know what the *Mona Lisa* looks like, right?"

"Of course. Everyone does."

"Imagine if someone ripped all the paint off it and turned that into a splatter painting."

"That'd be a travesty!" He looked horrified.

"Exactly. Xander is a splatter painting made from paint stolen from more worthy art. You're the *Mona Lisa*."

Alex looked stunned.

"Don't doubt it," Amanda said, lacing her other hand back through his. "You're a masterpiece that took a lot of thought, care, and work."

Alex seemed speechless.

Amanda turned on her power, and she smiled at the sight.

The other buildings were still shoved off to the edges. There were still piles of soot around a massive hole in the middle. But the hole was no longer a rift. Now it was a basement.

She had thought the soot was trash, but it wasn't. It was a building material.

One of the piles had been squeezed into a diamond brick.

It was the first brick of a new building named "marital love."